THE PENGUIN POETS

JOHN DONNE

John Donne was born into a Catholic family in 1572. After a conventional education at Hart Hall, Oxford, and Lincoln's Inn, he took part in the Earl of Essex's expedition to the Azores in 1597. He secretly married Anne More in December 1601, and was imprisoned by her father, Sir George, in the Fleet two months later. He was ordained priest in January 1615, and proceeded to a Doctorate of Divinity at Cambridge in April of that year. In 1621 he was made Dean of St Paul's in London, a post which he held until his death in 1631. He is famous for the sermons he preached in his later years as well as for his poems.

John Donne

A SELECTION OF HIS POETRY

EDITED WITH AN INTRODUCTION BY

JOHN HAYWARD

PENGUIN BOOKS

Penguin Books Ltd, Harmondsworth, Middlesex, England
Penguin Books Inc., 7110 Ambassador Road, Baltimore, Maryland 21207, U.S.A.
Penguin Books Australia Ltd, Ringwood, Victoria, Australia
Penguin Books Canada Ltd, 41 Steelcase Road West, Markham, Ontario, Canada
Penguin Books (N.Z.) Ltd, 182-190 Wairau Road, Auckland 10, New Zealand

—

First published 1950
Reprinted 1952, 1955, 1958, 1960, 1963, 1964, 1966, 1967, 1969, 1970,
1972, 1973, 1975

—

Made and printed in Great Britain
by Hunt Barnard Printing Ltd, Aylesbury
Set in Monotype Caslon

Introduction

ALTHOUGH Donne's reputation has suffered periodic eclipses, its brightness has steadily increased since the publication in 1633, two years after his death in the Deanery of St Paul's Cathedral, of the small quarto volume of poems entitled: POEMS BY J. D. WITH ELEGIES ON THE AUTHOR'S DEATH. Throughout the seventeenth century, though his popularity declined in favour of Cowley's insipid imitations, he continued to exercise a powerful influence on the poets of the so-called 'metaphysical' school, his poems being reprinted at regular intervals up to the Restoration, when Dryden began to impose a smoother technique on English verse. A new edition was called for as late as 1719 when the poems of his contemporaries and most of his disciples had long been out of print and generally neglected. Although the poetic taste of the eighteenth century was constitutionally allergic to his rugged style, it was at least capable of relishing his satire when it was ingeniously, if mistakenly, pre-digested and reconstituted by Pope. His exclusion from the early editions of Palgrave's *Golden Treasury* (for the single poem attributed to him there is not, in fact, his) and his minor place in the original *Oxford Book of English Verse* must not be accepted as evidence of the nineteenth century's indifference; for Coleridge's potent advocacy at the beginning of the century, Browning's in the middle, and towards the end the textual rehabilitation of such editors as Grosart, Norton and Chambers, steadily advanced Donne's claim to stand in the front rank of English poets. And it should be noted, in passing, that Victorian England, though it may have failed to appreciate Donne's poetry, did not misprize his sonorous prose:

the editorial and critical labours of Dean Alford and Dr Jessopp
are sufficient confirmation of this.

The first half of the present century, and the second quarter
of it, in particular, have been remarkable in literary history for
a broadening and deepening of interest in his poetry – an interest
now so widely diffused, though by no means so critical as it might
be, that it is difficult to believe that Donne will ever again fall
far into disrepute. His eminence at the present time owes much
to the great critical edition of his poems prepared by Sir Herbert
Grierson and published at Oxford in 1912. Later editions,
based on Grierson's definitive text, have served merely to extend
a popularity which has grown to such proportions that the
number of copies printed of the first issue of this latest selection
considerably exceeds the total of all the copies of all the editions
of Donne's poems printed since his death. This is an impressive
and provocative fact. It would be a mistake, however, to assume
that the supply of adequate texts to a reading public, greatly
enlarged by mass 'education', including such facilities as evening
classes, the W.E.A., and broadcast talks, has created this excep-
tional demand for the work of a poet who, according to one of
his friends, wrote 'all his best pieces ere he was twenty-five
years old', some 350 years ago. The demand has created the
supply, and this demand has arisen because Donne's poetry, more
than that of any of his contemporaries, not excepting even
Shakespeare's, seems to satisfy, or at least assuage, the appeten-
cies peculiar to the intelligence and sensibility of our own time.

It happens that we know more about Donne's career than we
do about the careers of any of the poets of his age, and can there-
fore confirm from his letters and other biographical sources, such
as Izaak Walton's *Life*, the nature of the experiences which
informed his thoughts and emotions. 'I had my first breeding
and conversation', he wrote, 'with men of suppressed and
afflicted religion, accustomed to the despite of death and hungry
of an imagined martyrdom.' Yet, even without such checks as

these, it would be clear enough that the problems and paradoxes of the human condition which he attempted to resolve in his poetry were not dissimilar in kind as well as in degree to those which beset us to-day. The apparent as well as the real difficulty of his verse – its allusiveness, its often puzzling ellipses, its argumentative tone, its irregular rhythms – has its counterpart in the verse of the poets who grew up between the two World Wars of the present century; it arises from the nature of the poetry, that is to say from the desire, however frustrating and frustrated, to achieve reconciliation of opposites, resolution of doubts, and integration of the world of reality with the world of the imagination. For Donne this meant the difficult reconciliation of the medieval with the modern conception of the universe; the resolution of personal doubts and anxieties arising, in his case, from religious and philosophic speculation (his family was Catholic and its members were grievously persecuted for their faith); the resolution of an inner conflict of carnal and spiritual longing – the incessant warring or at least sparring in his members of the 'Jack' Donne of the early love poems and the 'Doctor' Donne of the tremendous self-questionings cast in the form of sermons; and the integration of thought and feeling.

We think of Donne as a 'modern' poet just because he appears to think and feel as we do about the 'wearisome condition of humanity'; and we appreciate him the more because he does not sugar his 'songs and sonnets', as his contemporaries did, with a smooth and superficially delectable coating of poetic sweetness, but, breaking with a tradition as sharply as our own poets have with the post-Tennysonian insipidity of the 'Georgian Poets', uses verse as a medium for dialectic, for monologue, and for psychological analysis. This intellectual apprehension and expression of emotion, though it is often contorted by over-ingenious metaphors and allusions, and sometimes obscured by far-fetched 'conceits' (the overflow of what he called his 'hydroptique, immoderate desire for learning'), is surprisingly 'modern'. It is this quality of intellectuality, above all, which contracts the great differences between Donne's world and ours and establishes their points of contact. This is especially true of his sense of the value and mystery, in an uncompromising world, of personal relationships. If he is, as some would maintain, the greatest of English love-poets – the first to break clean away from the medieval ideal of *amour courtois* – he is also outstanding, perhaps unrivalled, as a poet of friendship – in his secular 'Verse Letters', 'Epithalamions' and 'Elegies', no less than in his 'Divine Poems', where he examines or 'anatomises' man's personal relationship with God.

Donne's poems, indeed, are largely the uninhibited and curiously annotated record – passionate or ironical, tender or teasing, as the case may be – of many love-affairs before marriage and many life-long friendships. Of the former we know only as much as he allows us to infer, which amounts to little more than an occasional disclosure of ways and means to a desired end – in the earliest poems, mere physical pleasure, or as he calls it, 'the sport': 'Let me love none, no, but the sport'; in the later a more romantic, more detached longing for a satisfactory sexual relationship. We can only guess which of the 'Songs and Sonets' and 'Elegies' were written for and about Anne More, whom he courted in secret while he was living and employed as a secretary in her uncle's house, and with whom he improvidently eloped. Of his friendships we know more than enough to prove how constantly he loved and was loved by his friends – Henry Wotton, Christopher and Samuel Brooke (who connived in his runaway marriage and shared imprisonment with him as a result), Henry Goodyer, Robert Drury, the Earl of Dorset, Lucy Bedford, Magdalen Herbert, Elizabeth Huntingdon, and many more. Nothing is known about his emotional attitude to his father, who died when he was four years old, or to his mother, who remarried almost immediately; but his silence about his mother is perhaps of some significance. The early poems and letters suggest that he was excellent company, at times perhaps too clever by half, yet uncommonly witty and well-informed, much given to highly sophisticated fantasy and with a keen critical appreciation of the ridiculous. His satires show that he did not suffer fools gladly, though he would doubtless have suffered more if he had not been able to vent his intolerance in verse. Tradition has it that when he came down from Oxford and lived in chambers in Lincoln's Inn he was 'not dissolute but very neat; a great Visitor of Ladies, a great Frequenter of Plays, a great writer of conceited Verses'. The charge that his youth was unduly licentious and disorderly cannot be sustained. His unabashed delight in describing sensual pleasure may shock the prudish, but will not surprise those who recognize in this gratification of the senses an essential quality of Renaissance man. There is, one feels, more than a tenuous resemblance between Donne and Hamlet.

Donne did not suddenly sober down when he took Holy Orders at the age of forty-three. The passion with which he had courted those whom he called his 'profane mistresses' became sublimated in a fearful longing for union with God. In his later years the lust of the spirit demanded satisfaction no less than the lust of the flesh had done in the heyday of the blood. His poems, however, are not an expression of simple delight in the desires and satisfactions either of the senses or of the spirit. Donne did not sing for joy as Herrick did of the one and Herbert of the other. The inquisitiveness and speculations of his 'riddling, intricated, perplexed, labyrinthical soul' went far deeper than theirs; and there is also a sombre, uneasy, saturnine cast to his genius – 'a fervent and gloomy sublimity' as de Quincey calls it – which marks him out from his contemporaries, even from such tragic writers as Webster and Tourneur. The temper of the times doubtless contributed much to the forming of this disposition. It is one with which we can the more readily sympathize, because we in our time have experienced what Donne experienced in his: the breaking-up of the old order of things;

the disturbing progress of scientific discovery; the growth of scepticism; apprehension of sudden or violent death; persecution and intolerance. 'The new philosophy (he wrote) calls all in doubt.' The revelation that the earth is not the centre of the universe was doubtless as profoundly unsettling to the thoughtful men of Donne's generation as the implications of nuclear fission are to us.

Donne's verse is intermittently overcast with dark imagery and charged with queer scientific tropes which reflect obliquely his philosophic doubts and anxiety. His art consists in finding an emotional equivalent, a correspondence, as it were, for these intellectual gropings; in creating, by means of sensuous images, a single poetic image of the material, sensible, and spiritual world of his experience. Faith and reason are perpetually in conflict in his verse and both are reinforced by supporting evidence drawn from patristic and scholastic writers. The weight of his learning is formidable and at times indeed overwhelming; but while it is true that it is impossible to understand fully the significance of some passages in his poems without some familiarity with his sources – the second stanza of 'Aire and Angels' is a good example – not even a devoted reader should suppose that he must emulate Donne's learning in order to understand him. It would indeed be unprofitable to attempt to do so. For the *poetry* is never incomprehensible, and the thrill of responding to it (for Donne is pre-eminently a thrilling writer in prose as well as in verse) will not be measurably increased by study of medieval theology and philosophy.

When Ben Jonson, Donne's friend and one of the earliest of his critical admirers, visited William Drummond at Hawthornden during the winter of 1618 he seems to have alluded to Donne more frequently than to any other poet of the period, although all his best poems, at that date, were known only from manuscript copies in private circulation. And yet Drummond noted down that his guest considered 'John Donne the first poet in the world in some things'. Jonson did not praise indiscriminately or lightly; he would not tolerate uncritical adulation even of his admired Shakespeare; and, as we shall see, he was doubtful whether Donne's merits outweighed his defects. But he recognized that Donne was, at his best, incomparable, and that verdict has stood for over 300 years. It is tempting to suggest a possible ambiguity in Jonson's *obiter dictum*, to infer that in his estimation Donne was the first poet in the world to have written some kinds of verse. If Jonson had intended this and had had in mind Donne's technical innovations and, above all, his mastery of the difficult art, practised by Shakespeare in his later plays, of finding a poetical equivalent for the rhythm of conversation, it would explain his further remark to Drummond – 'that Donne, for not keeping of accent, deserved hanging'. Certainly Donne's lack of conventional smoothness, one might say his deliberate disregard for the orthodox poetical proprieties of his age, must have seemed very awkward to ears attuned to Spenser and the formal sonneteers. To an older generation, brought up on the sonnets and blank verse of Wyatt and Lord Surrey – themselves innovators less than fifty years before – Donne's uncouthness must have seemed as reprehensible or at least as unsympathetic as Hardy's peculiar ruggedness did to a generation accustomed to the mellifluous flow of Tennyson's and Swinburne's verse, or as the rhythms of *The Waste Land* to the admirers of Rupert Brooke and Flecker.

Coleridge was the first to point out a purpose and significance in Donne's metric. True, in a lighter mood, he turned an epigram on the subject:

ON DONNE'S POETRY

With Donne, whose muse on dromedary trots,
Wreathe iron pokers into true-love knots;
Rhyme's sturdy cripple, fancy's maze and clue,
Wit's forge and fire-blast, meaning's press and screw.

But Coleridge knew how to ride the dromedary and, in a few words, explained how it must be done. 'To read Dryden, Pope, etc,' he wrote, 'you need only count syllables; but to read Donne you must measure *Time*, and discover the time of each word by the sense of Passion.' He expressed the same thing in rather more specific terms, in a note on the *Song:* 'Sweetest love, I do not goe' (p. 32), the most regular of all Donne's poems: 'This beautiful and perfect poem,' he says, 'proves by its title "Song", that *all* Donne's Poems are equally *metrical*, though *smoothness*, that is to say the metre necessitating the proper reading, be deemed appropriate to *songs;* but, in Poems where the Author *thinks*, and expects the Readers to do so, the sense must be understood in order to ascertain the metre.'

To read Donne aright is largely a matter of practice, which may entail a good deal of perseverance and patience before pleasure is assured. The punctuation is an important guide, and Donne intended it to perform the same service as rests in musical notation. Experience in reading will reveal, progressively, the correct value of each stressed word, and recognition of these values leads, almost insensibly, to an understanding of the metrical scheme, which is seldom confined by the rhythm of a single line but extends into paragraphs. Where the sense is obscure and the metre consequently uncertain, it is often helpful to read the whole poem aloud, for subtleties of syntax and rhythm which escape the eye may sometimes be caught in the ear or on the tongue. Some harshness and dissonance, however, will remain, and the most sensitive ear will fail to resolve some of Donne's rasping cadences; for, even when allowance is made for the fact that he did not correct or revise his poems for publication, and that his editors have had to establish his text from misprinted originals, it is evident that he was more interested in sense than in sound and careless about their co-ordination. Almost all his poems are dramatic monologues uttered in a mood of passionate apprehension. The passion draws together the words of common speech and attempts sometimes to fuse the incoherent. Donne did not stop to recast or refine. There is no 'poetic diction', no use of polish, no compromise with the kind of music to the accompaniment of which the lyrics of Donne's contemporaries were commonly sung. 'It is seldom', says Saintsbury, 'that even for a few lines, seldom that for a few stanzas, the power of the furnace is equal to the volumes of ore and fuel that are thrust into it. But the fire is always there – over-tasked, over-mastered for a time, but never choked or extinguished; and ever and anon from gaps in the smouldering mass there breaks forth such a sudden flow of pure molten metal, such a flower of incandescense, as not even in the very greatest poets of all can be ever surpassed or often rivalled.'

'The first poet in the world in some things.' Yet Jonson also told Drummond that Donne 'for not being understood would perish'. Time has disproved that assertion, but not because posterity has been more apt to understand him than his contemporaries were. If Donne has survived the misrepresentation of his imitators, who brought the practice of 'metaphysical' verse into disrepute, and the denunciation of Dr Johnson, it is because appreciation of his poems is not a matter so much of understanding as of feeling. It is in this sense that the statement, 'the *poetry* is never incomprehensible', must be accepted. In other words, it is possible to feel what he means even when it is difficult, perhaps impossible, to understand his literal meaning. There are, of course, degrees of appreciation; and the reader who can recognize the overtones and undertones of Donne's irony, who can follow his subtle but involuted dialectic, and can discount a certain amount of what seems to us tasteless wit, will enjoy him more than one who is fascinated only by his superficial brilliance and curious power to charm. To some readers his poetry may seem to be no more than an extravagant essay in the baroque, a fantastic conglomeration of fact and fancy in which the technique of chiaroscuro is ingeniously used to cast fitful high-lights and shadows across a woman's breasts, a *memento mori*, a mandrake root, 'a bracelet of bright hair about the bone'. To others the discovery of Donne, whether in his poetry or his prose, secular as well as divine, will be the recognition of a kindred spirit – and, one may add, of a kindred flesh. Such readers are relatively more numerous to-day than at any time since Donne's death because his poetry expresses for us our own hopes and fears of an analogous human condition, with all its situations of foreboding and frustration and its occasions for irony and dismay, created by our personal relationships and social responsibilities, by our sense of insecurity in a world in which private and public morality has failed to keep pace with scientific 'progress', and by our spiritual misgivings and perplexities in a world whose values are predominantly materialistic.

JOHN HAYWARD

Acknowledgements

I wish to thank Miss Helen Gardner for valuable criticism and advice; and Sir Edward Marsh for reading some of the book in proof.

Note on the Text

THE present text is substantially the same as the one I prepared for the Nonesuch Press (*Complete Poetry and Selected Prose*), and is based upon the original editions of 1633 and 1635 – the primary printed authorities – and a number of textually important MS collections which were in circulation while Donne was still alive. It has been amended in a few places in the light of later knowledge or more mature consideration. With one exception the order of the poems follows that of the Nonesuch edition. The approximate dates of their composition are given in the list of Contents. The original spelling and punctuation have been retained and altered only where the sense seemed likely to be obscured[1]. A reader coming to Donne for the first time may be puzzled by his system of punctuation. But familiarity will breed respect for his deliberate use of stopping (including the apostrophe) as a kind of musical notation to assist the reader's appreciation of the subtle nuances of his metric. The 'Epigrams', the 'Progresse of the Soule', the Latin verses and translations have been omitted in their entirety, while the 'Anniversaries' are represented only by extracts, sufficient indeed to reveal the curious fascination and 'pregnant phansie', but not the tediousness of these long and involuted panegyrics. The other omissions from the canon are neither excessive nor, it is to be hoped, important enough to amount to a serious deprivation.

If this selection should stimulate the reader to a closer study of the text and significance of Donne's poetry, his indispensable guide must always be Grierson's definitive edition and commentary (Oxford, 1912, 2 volumes). J. H.

1. To avoid confusion, quotation marks have been supplied in the 'Satyrs'.

Chronological Table

Born in London (probably between 22 Jan. and 12 Feb.)	1572
Matriculated Hart Hall, Oxford	23 October 1584
Admitted to Lincoln's Inn	6 May 1592
? Foreign Travel	? 1594–6
Foreign Service with the Earl of Essex	June 1596
The Azores Expedition (The Islands Voyage)	August 1597
Secretary to Sir Thomas Egerton	c. 1598–1602
Secretly married to Anne More	December 1601
Imprisoned in the Fleet by Sir George More	February 1601–2
Marriage ratified	April 1602
Residence with Sir Francis Wooley at Pyrford	1602–4
Residence at Mitcham	1605–9
Employed by Thomas Morton	c. 1605–7
Pseudo-Martyr published	January 1610
Hon. M.A., Oxford	17 April 1610
Residence at Drury House	1610
Ignatius his Conclave published	1611
An Anatomy of the World (*The First Anniversarie*) published	1611
The First Anniversarie reprinted, with *The Second Anniversarie*	1612
Continental Travel with Sir Robert Drury	November 1611–September 1612
Ordained priest	23 January 1614–5
Doctor of Divinity, Cambridge	April 1615
First surviving Sermon (To the Queen at Greenwich)	30 April 1615
Presented to the livings of Keyston and Sevenoaks	1614–5
Reader in Divinity to the Benchers of Lincoln's Inn	October 1617–February 1622
First Sermon preached at Paul's Cross	24 March 1617
Death of his wife, Anne Donne	15 August 1617
With Lord Doncaster's Embassy to Germany	May 1619–December 1620

Dean of Saint Paul's	19 November 1621
Seriously ill. Composition of *Devotions* (pub. 1624)	Winter 1623
Appointed to St Dunstan's in the West	March 1624
Plague in London. Retires to Magdalen Danvers's house in Chelsea	August 1625
Death's Duell preached	12 February 1630–1
Dies in London	31 March 1631
First collected edition of *Poems*	1633
LXXX Sermons published	1640
Biathanatos published	[1646]
Fifty Sermons published	1649
Letters published	1651
Essayes in Divinity published	1651
XXVI Sermons published	1661

Contents

(The dates are those of composition)

SONGS AND SONETS

(mainly *c.* 1593–1601)

ELEGIES

EPITHALAMIONS

SATYRES
(c. 1593-7)

VERSE LETTERS

ANNIVERSARIES, EPICEDES AND OBSEQUIES

The Poems

SONGS AND SONETS

THE GOOD-MORROW

I wonder by my troth, what thou, and I
Did, till we lov'd? were we not wean'd till then?
But suck'd on countrey pleasures, childishly?
Or snorted we in the seaven sleepers den?
T'was so; But this, all pleasures fancies bee.
If ever any beauty I did see,
Which I desir'd, and got, t'was but a dreame of thee.

And now good morrow to our waking soules,
Which watch not one another out of feare;
For love, all love of other sights controules,
And makes one little roome, an every where.
Let sea-discoverers to new worlds have gone,
Let Maps to other, worlds on worlds have showne,
Let us possesse one world, each hath one, and is one.

My face in thine eye, thine in mine appeares,
And true plaine hearts doe in the faces rest,
Where can we finde two better hemispheares
Without sharpe North, without declining West?
What ever dyes, was not mixt equally;
If our two loves be one, or, thou and I
Love so alike, that none doe slacken, none can die.

SONG

Goe, and catche a falling starre,
   Get with child a mandrake roote,
Tell me, where all past yeares are,
   Or who cleft the Divels foot,
Teach me to heare Mermaides singing,
   Or to keep off envies stinging,
          And finde
          What winde
Serves to advance an honest minde.

If thou beest borne to strange sights,
   Things invisible to see,
Ride ten thousand daies and nights,
   Till age snow white haires on thee,
Thou, when thou retorn'st, wilt tell mee
All strange wonders that befell thee,
          And sweare
          No where
Lives a woman true, and faire.

If thou findst one, let mee know,
   Such a Pilgrimage were sweet;
Yet doe not, I would not goe,
   Though at next doore wee might meet,
Though shee were true, when you met her,
And last, till you write your letter,
          Yet shee
          Will bee
False, ere I come, to two, or three.

WOMANS CONSTANCY

Now thou hast lov'd me one whole day,
To morrow when thou leav'st, what wilt thou say?
Wilt thou then Antedate some new made vow?
      Or say that now
We are not just those persons, which we were?
Or, that oathes made in reverentiall feare
Of Love, and his wrath, any may forsweare?
Or, as true deaths, true maryages untie,
So lovers contracts, images of those,
Binde but till sleep, deaths image, them unloose?
       Or, your owne end to Justifie,
For having purpos'd change, and falsehood; you
Can have no way but falsehood to be true?
Vaine lunatique, against these scapes I could
      Dispute, and conquer, if I would,
      Which I abstaine to doe,
For by to morrow, I may thinke so too.

THE UNDERTAKING

I have done one braver thing
   Than all the *Worthies* did,
And yet a braver thence doth spring,
   Which is, to keepe that hid.

It were but madness now t'impart
   The skill of specular stone,
When he which can have learn'd the art
   To cut it, can finde none.

So, if I now should utter this,
   Others (because no more
Such stuffe to worke upon, there is,)
   Would love but as before.

But he who lovelinesse within
   Hath found, all outward loathes,
For he who colour loves, and skinne,
   Loves but their oldest clothes.

If, as I have, you also doe
   Vertue'attir'd in woman see,
And dare love that, and say so too,
   And forget the Hee and Shee;

And if this love, though placed so,
   From prophane men you hide,
Which will no faith on this bestow,
    Or, if they doe, deride:

Then you have done a braver thing
   Than all the *Worthies* did;
And a braver thence will spring,
   Which is, to keepe that hid.

THE SUNNE RISING

Busie old foole, unruly Sunne,
   Why dost thou thus,
Through windowes, and through curtains call on us?
Must to thy motions lovers seasons run?
   Sawcy pedantique wretch, goe chide
   Late schoole boyes and sowre prentices,

Goe tell Court-huntsmen, that the King will ride,
 Call countrey ants to harvest offices;
Love, all alike, no season knowes, nor clyme,
Nor houres, dayes, moneths, which are the rags of time.

  Thy beames, so reverend, and strong
   Why shouldst thou thinke?
I could eclipse and cloud them with a winke,
But that I would not lose her sight so long:
  If her eyes have not blinded thine,
   Looke, and to morrow late, tell mee,
 Whether both the'India's of spice and Myne
 Be where thou leftst them, or lie here with mee.
Aske for those Kings whom thou saw'st yesterday,
And thou shalt heare, All here in one bed lay.

  She'is all States, and all Princes, I,
   Nothing else is.
Princes doe but play us; compar'd to this,
All honor's mimique; All wealth alchimie.
  Thou sunne art halfe as happy'as wee,
   In that the world's contracted thus;
 Thine age askes ease, and since thy duties bee
 To warme the world, that's done in warming us.
Shine here to us, and thou art every where;
This bed thy center is, these walls, thy spheare.

LOVES USURY

For every houre that thou wilt spare mee now,
  I will allow,
Usurious God of Love, twenty to thee,
When with my browne, my gray haires equall bee;

Till then, Love, let my body raigne, and let
Mee travell, sojourne, snatch, plot, have, forget,
Resume my last yeares relict: thinke that yet
      We'had never met.

Let mee thinke any rivalls letter mine,
      And at next nine
Keepe midnights promise; mistake by the way
The maid, and tell the Lady of that delay;
Onely let mee love none, no, but the sport;
From country grasse, to comfitures of Court,
Or cities quelque choses, let report
      My minde transport.

This bargaine's good; if when I'am old, I bee
      Inflam'd by thee,
If thine owne honour, or my shame, or paine,
Thou covet most, at that age thou shalt gaine.
Doe thy will then, then subject and degree,
And fruit of love, Love I submit to thee,
Spare mee till then, I'll beare it, though she bee
      One that loves mee.

THE CANONIZATION

For Godsake hold your tongue, and let me love,
  Or chide my palsie, or my gout,
My five gray haires, or ruin'd fortune flout,
    With wealth your state, your minde with Arts improve,
    Take you a course, get you a place,
    Observe his honour, or his grace,
Or the Kings reall, or his stamped face
  Contemplate, what you will, approve,
  So you will let me love.

Alas, alas, who's injur'd by my love?
   What merchants ships have my sighs drown'd?
Who saies my teares have overflow'd his ground?
   When did my colds a forward spring remove?
     When did the heats which my veines fill
     Adde one more to the plaguie Bill?
Soldiers finde warres, and Lawyers finde out still
   Litigious men, which quarrels move,
   Though she and I do love.

Call us what you will, wee are made such by love;
   Call her one, mee another flye,
We'are Tapers too, and at our owne cost die,
   And wee in us finde the'Eagle and the Dove.
     The Phœnix ridle hath more wit
     By us, we two being one, are it.
So, to one neutrall thing both sexes fit,
   Wee dye and rise the same, and prove
   Mysterious by this love.

Wee can dye by it, if not live by love,
   And if unfit for tombs and hearse
Our legend bee, it will be fit for verse;
   And if no peece of Chronicle wee prove,
     We'll build in sonnets pretty roomes;
     As well a well wrought urne becomes
The greatest ashes, as halfe-acre tombes,
   And by these hymnes, all shall approve
   Us *Canoniz'd* for Love:

And thus invoke us; You whom reverend love
   Made one anothers hermitage;
You, to whom love was peace, that now is rage;
   Who did the whole worlds soule contract, and drove

Into the glasses of your eyes
(So made such mirrors, and such spies,
That they did all to you epitomize,)
Countries, Townes, Courts: Beg from above
A patterne of your love!

THE TRIPLE FOOLE

I am two fooles, I know,
For loving, and for saying so
    In whining Poëtry;
But where's that wiseman, that would not be I,
    If she would not deny?
Then as th'earths inward narrow crooked lanes
Do purge sea waters fretfull salt away,
    I thought, if I could draw my paines,
Through Rimes vexation, I should them allay.
Griefe brought to numbers cannot be so fierce,
For, he tames it, that fetters it in verse.

But when I have done so,
Some man, his art and voice to show,
    Doth Set and sing my paine,
And, by delighting many, frees againe
    Griefe, which verse did restraine.
To Love, and Griefe tribute of Verse belongs,
But not of such as pleases when'tis read,
    Both are increased by such songs:
For both their triumphs so are published,
And I, which was two fooles, do so grow three;
Who are a little wise, the best fooles bee.

LOVERS INFINITENESSE

If yet I have not all thy love,
Deare, I shall never have it all,
I cannot breathe one other sigh, to move,
Nor can intreat one other teare to fall,
And all my treasure, which should purchase thee,
Sighs, teares, and oathes, and letters I have spent.
Yet no more can be due to mee,
Than at the bargaine made was ment,
If then thy gift of love were partiall,
That some to mee, some should to others fall,
   Deare, I shall never have Thee All.

Or if then thou gavest mee all,
All was but All, which thou hadst then;
But if in thy heart, since, there be or shall,
New love created bee, by other men,
Which have their stocks intire, and can in teares,
In sighs, in oathes, and letters outbid mee,
This new love may beget new feares,
For, this love was not vowed by thee.
And yet it was, thy gift being generall,
The ground, thy heart is mine, what ever shall
   Grow there, deare, I should have it all.

Yet I would not have all yet,
Hee that hath all can have no more,
And since my love doth every day admit
New growth, thou shouldst have new rewards in store;
Thou canst not every day give me thy heart,
If thou canst give it, then thou never gavest it:
Loves riddles are, that though thy heart depart,
It stayes at home, and thou with losing savest it:

But wee will have a way more liberall,
Than changing hearts, to joyne them, so wee shall
　　Be one, and one anothers All.

SONG

　　Sweetest love, I do not goe,
　　　　For weariness of thee,
　　Nor in hope the world can show
　　　　A fitter Love for mee;
　　　　　　But since that I
　　Must dye at last, 'tis best,
　　To use my selfe in jest
　　　　Thus by fain'd deaths to dye;

　　Yesternight the Sunne went hence,
　　　　And yet is here to day,
　　He hath no desire nor sense,
　　　　Nor halfe so short a way:
　　　　　　Then feare not mee,
　　But beleeve that I shall make
　　Speedier journeyes, since I take
　　　　More wings and spurres than hee.

　　O how feeble is mans power,
　　　　That if good fortune fall,
　　Cannot adde another houre,
　　　　Nor a lost houre recall!
　　　　　　But come bad chance,
　　And wee joyne to'it our strength,
　　And wee teach it art and length,
　　　　It selfe o'r us to'advance.

When thou sigh'st, thou sigh'st not winde,
    But sigh'st my soule away,
When thou weep'st, unkindly kinde,
    My lifes blood doth decay.
        It cannot bee
That thou lov'st mee, as thou say'st,
If in thine my life thou waste,
    That art the best of mee.

Let not thy divining heart
    Forethinke me any ill,
Destiny may take thy part,
    And may thy feares fulfill;
        But thinke that wee
Are but turn'd aside to sleepe;
They who one another keepe
    Alive, ne'r parted bee.

THE LEGACIE

When I dyed last, and, Deare, I dye
    As often as from thee I goe,
    Though it be but an houre agoe,
And Lovers houres be full eternity,
I can remember yet, that I
    Something did say, and something did bestow;
Though I be dead, which sent mee, I should be
Mine owne executor and Legacie.

I heard mee say, Tell her anon,
    That my selfe, (that is you, not I,)
    Did kill me, and when I felt mee dye,
I bid mee send my heart, when I was gone,

But I alas could there finde none,
 When I had ripp'd me, 'and search'd where
  hearts did lye;
It kill'd mee againe, that I who still was true,
In life, in my last Will should cozen you.

Yet I found something like a heart,
 But colours it, and corners had,
 If was not good, it was not bad,
It was intire to none, and few had part.
As good as could be made by art
 It seem'd; and therefore for our losses sad,
I meant to send this heart in stead of mine,
But oh, no man could hold it, for twas thine.

A FEAVER

Oh doe not die, for I shall hate
 All women so, when thou art gone,
That thee I shall not celebrate,
 When I remember, thou wast one.

But yet thou canst not die, I know,
 To leave this world behinde, is death,
But when thou from this world wilt goe,
 The whole world vapors with thy breath.

Or if, when thou, the worlds soule, goest,
 It stay, tis but thy carkasse then,
The fairest woman, but thy ghost,
 But corrupt wormes, the worthyest men.

O wrangling schooles, that search what fire
   Shall burne this world, had none the wit
Unto this knowledge to aspire,
   That this her feaver might be it?

And yet she cannot wast by this,
   Nor long beare this torturing wrong,
For such corruption needfull is
   To fuell such a feaver long.

These burning fits but meteors bee,
   Whose matter in thee is soone spent.
Thy beauty,'and all parts, which are thee,
   Are unchangeable firmament.

Yet 'twas of my minde, seising thee,
   Though it in thee cannot persever.
For I had rather owner bee
   Of thee one houre, than all else ever.

AIRE AND ANGELS

Twice or thrice had I loved thee,
Before I knew thy face or name;
So in a voice, so in a shapelesse flame,
Angells affect us oft, and worship'd bee;
   Still when, to where thou wert, I came,
Some lovely glorious nothing I did see.
   But since my soule, whose child love is,
Takes limmes of flesh, and else could nothing doe,
   More subtile than the parent is,
Love must not be, but take a body too,
   And therefore what thou wert, and who,

I bid Love aske, and now
That it assume thy body, I allow,
And fixe it selfe in thy lip, eye, and brow.

Whilst thus to ballast love, I thought,
And so more steddily to have gone,
With wares which would sinke admiration,
I saw, I had loves pinnace overfraught,
    Ev'ry thy haire for love to worke upon
Is much too much, some fitter must be sought;
    For, nor in nothing, nor in things
Extreme, and scatt'ring bright, can love inhere;
    Then as an Angell, face, and wings
Of aire, not pure as it, yet pure doth weare,
    So thy love may be my loves spheare;
        Just such disparitie
As is twixt Aire and Angells puritie,
'Twixt womens love, and mens will ever bee.

BREAKE OF DAY

'Tis true, 'tis day; what though it be?
O wilt thou therefore rise from me?
Why should we rise? because 'tis light?
Did we lie downe, because 'twas night?
Love which in spight of darknesse brought us hether,
Should in despight of light keepe us together.

Light hath no tongue, but is all eye;
If it could speake as well as spie,
This were the worst, that it could say,
That being well, I faine would stay,
And that I lov'd my heart and honor so,
That I would not from him, that had them, goe.

Must businesse thee from hence remove?
Oh, that's the worst disease of love,
The poore, the foule, the false, love can
Admit, but not the busied man.
He which hath businesse, and makes love, doth doe
Such wrong, as when a maryed man doth wooe.

THE ANNIVERSARIE

All Kings, and all their favorites,
   All glory of honors, beauties, wits,
The Sun it selfe, which makes times, as they passe,
Is elder by a yeare, now, than it was
When thou and I first one another saw:
All other things, to their destruction draw,
   Only our love hath no decay;
This, no to morrow hath, nor yesterday,
Running it never runs from us away,
But truly keepes his first, last, everlasting day.

   Two graves must hide thine and my coarse,
   If one might, death were no divorce.
Alas, as well as other Princes, wee,
(Who Prince enough in one another bee,)
Must leave at last in death, these eyes, and eares,
Oft fed with true oathes, and with sweet salt teares;
   But soules where nothing dwells but love
(All other thoughts being inmates) then shall prove
This, or a love increased there above,
When bodies to their graves, soules from their graves
   remove.

And then wee shall be throughly blest,
But wee no more, than all the rest;
Here upon earth, we'are Kings, and none but wee
Can be such Kings, nor of such subjects bee.
Who is so safe as wee? where none can doe
Treason to us, except one of us two.

True and false feares let us refraine,
Let us love nobly, and live, and adde againe
Yeares and yeares unto yeares, till we attaine
To write threescore: this is the second of our raigne.

A VALEDICTION: OF MY NAME, IN THE WINDOW

I

My name engrav'd herein,
Doth contribute my firmnesse to this glasse,
    Which, ever since that charme, hath beene
    As hard, as that which grav'd it, was;
Thine eye will give it price enough, to mock
    The diamonds of either rock.

II

    'Tis much that glasse should bee
As all confessing, and through-shine as I,
    'Tis more, that it shewes thee to thee,
    And cleare reflects thee to thine eye.
But all such rules, loves magique can undoe,
    Here you see mee, and I am you.

III

    As no one point, nor dash,
Which are but accessaries to this name,
    The showers and tempests can outwash,
    So shall all times finde mee the same;

You this intirenesse better may fulfill,
    Who have the patterne with you still.

IIII

    Or if too hard and deepe
This learning be, for a scratch'd name to teach,
    It, as a given deaths head keepe,
    Lovers mortalitie to preach,
Or thinke this ragged bony name to bee
    My ruinous Anatomie.

V

    Then, as all my soules bee,
Emparadis'd in you, (in whom alone
    I understand, and grow and see,)
    The rafters of my body, bone
Being still with you, the Muscle, Sinew, and Veine,
    Which tile this house, will come againe.

VI

    Till my returne, repaire
And recompact my scattered body so.
    As all the vertuous powers which are
    Fix'd in the starres, are said to flow
Into such characters, as graved bee
    When these starres have supremacie:

VII

    So since this name was cut
When love and griefe their exaltation had,
    No doore 'gainst this names influence shut;
    As much more loving, as more sad,
'Twill make thee; and thou shouldst, till I returne,
    Since I die daily, daily mourne.

VIII

When thy inconsiderate hand
Flings ope this casement, with my trembling name,
   To looke on one, whose wit or land,
   New battry to thy heart may frame,
Then thinke this name alive, and that thou thus
     In it offendst my Genius.

IX

And when thy melted maid,
Corrupted by thy Lover's gold, and page,
   His letter at thy pillow'hath laid,
   Disputed it, and tam'd thy rage,
And thou begin'st to thaw towards him, for this,
     May my name step in, and hide his.

X

And if this treason goe
To an overt act, and that thou write againe;
   In superscribing, this name flow
   Into thy fancy, from the pane.
So, in forgetting thou remembrest right,
     And unaware to mee shalt write.

XI

But glasse, and lines must bee,
No meanes our firme substantiall love to keepe;
   Neere death inflicts this lethargie,
   And this I murmure in my sleepe;
Impute this idle talke, to that I goe,
     For dying men talke often so.

TWICKNAM GARDEN[1]

Blasted with sighs, and surrounded with teares,
   Hither I come to seeke the spring,
   And at mine eyes, and at mine eares,
Receive such balmes, as else cure every thing;
   But O, selfe traytor, I do bring
The spider love, which transubstantiates all,
   And can convert Manna to gall,
And that this place may thoroughly be thought
   True Paradise, I have the serpent brought.

'Twere wholsomer for mee, that winter did
   Benight the glory of this place,
   And that a grave frost did forbid
These trees to laugh, and mocke mee to my face;
   But that I may not this disgrace
Indure, nor yet leave loving, Love let mee
   Some senslesse peece of this place bee;
Make me a mandrake, so I may groane here,
   Or a stone fountaine weeping out my yeare.

Hither with christall vyals, lovers come,
   And take my teares, which are loves wine,
   And try your mistresse Teares at home,
For all are false, that tast not just like mine;
   Alas, hearts do not in eyes shine,
Nor can you more judge womans thoughts by teares,
   Than by her shadow, what she weares.
O perverse sexe, where none is true but shee,
   Who's therefore true, because her truth kills mee.

1. Donne was a frequent guest of his friend and patroness Lucy, Countess of
Bedford, when she and her husband lived at Twickenham from 1608 to
1617. Sir William Temple praised her skill and taste for gardening.

A VALEDICTION: OF THE BOOKE

I'll tell thee now (deare Love) what thou shalt doe
    To anger destiny, as she doth us,
    How I shall stay, though she Esloygne[1] me thus
And how posterity shall know it too;
        How thine may out-endure
        Sybills glory, and obscure
        Her[2] who from Pindar could allure,
    And her,[3] through whose helpe *Lucan* is not lame,
And her,[4] whose booke (they say) *Homer* did finde, and
    name.

Study our manuscripts, those Myriades
    Of letters, which have past twixt thee and mee,
    Thence write our Annals, and in them will bee
To all whom loves subliming fire invades,
        Rule and example found;
        There, the faith of any ground
        No schismatique will dare to wound,
    That sees, how Love this grace to us affords,
To make, to keep, to use, to be these his Records.

This Booke, as long-liv'd as the elements,
    Or as the worlds forme, this all-graved tome
    In cypher writ, or new made Idiome,
Wee for loves clergie only'are instruments:
        When this booke is made thus,
        Should againe the ravenous
        Vandals and Goths inundate us,

1. This form was current throughout the seventeenth century.
2. Corinna, who out-rivalled Pindar.
3. Lucan's wife, who helped to correct his *Pharsalia*.
4. According to ancient tradition she was either (i) Phantasia of Memphis, or (ii) Helena, daughter of Musaeus.

Learning were safe; in this our Universe
Schooles might learne Sciences, Spheares Musick, Angels
     Verse.

Here Loves Divines, (since all Divinity
  Is love or wonder) may finde all they seeke,
  Whether abstract spirituall love they like,
Their Soules exhal'd with what they do not see,
    Or, loth so to amuze
    Faiths infirmitie, they chuse
    Something which they may see and use;
  For, though minde be the heaven, where love doth sit,
Beauty a convenient type may be to figure it.

Here more than in their bookes may Lawyers finde,
  Both by what titles Mistresses are ours,
  And how prerogative these states devours,
Transferr'd from Love himselfe, to womankinde.
    Who though from heart, and eyes,
    They exact great subsidies,
    Forsake him who on them relies,
  And for the cause, honour, or conscience give,
Chimeraes, vaine as they, or their prerogative.

Here Statesmen, (or of them, they which can reade,)
  May of their occupation finde the grounds:
  Love and their art alike it deadly wounds,
If to consider what 'tis, one proceed,
    In both they doe excell
    Who the present governe well,
    Whose weaknesse none doth, or dares tell;
  In this thy booke, such will their nothing see,
As in the Bible some can finde out Alchimy.

Thus vent thy thoughts; abroad I'll studie thee,
  As he removes farre off, that great heights takes;
  How great love is, presence best tryall makes,
But absence tryes how long this love will bee;
    To take a latitude
    Sun, or starres, are fitliest view'd
    At their brightest, but to conclude
Of longitudes, what other way have wee,
But to marke when, and where the darke eclipses bee?

LOVES GROWTH

I scarce beleeve my love to be so pure
    As I had thought it was,
    Because it doth endure
Vicissitude, and season, as the grasse;
Me thinkes I lyed all winter, when I swore,
My love was infinite, if spring make'it more.
But if this medicine, love, which cures all sorrow
With more, not onely bee no quintessence,
But mixt of all stuffes, paining soule, or sense,
And of the Sunne his working vigour borrow,
Love's not so pure, and abstract, as they use
To say, which have no Mistresse but their Muse,
But as all else, being elemented too,
Love sometimes would contemplate, sometimes do.

And yet no greater, but more eminent,
    Love by the Spring is growne;
    As, in the firmament,
Starres by the Sunne are not inlarg'd, but showne.
Gentle love deeds, as blossomes on a bough,
From loves awakened root do bud out now.

If, as in water stir'd more circles bee
Produc'd by one, love such additions take,
Those like so many spheares, but one heaven make,
For, they are all concentrique unto thee.
And though each spring doe adde to love new heate,
As princes doe in times of action get
New taxes, and remit them not in peace,
No winter shall abate the springs encrease.

THE DREAME

Deare love, for nothing lesse than thee
Would I have broke this happy dreame,
    It was a theame
For reason, much too strong for phantasie,
Therefore thou wakd'st me wisely; yet
My Dreame thou brok'st not, but continued'st it,
Thou art so truth, that thoughts of thee suffice,
To make dreames truths; and fables histories;
Enter these armes, for since thou thoughtst it best,
Not to dreame all my dreame, let's act the rest.

As lightning, or a Tapers light,
Thine eyes, and not thy noise wak'd mee;
    Yet I thought thee
(For thou lovest truth) an Angell, at first sight,
But when I saw thou sawest my heart,
And knew'st my thoughts, beyond an Angels art,
When thou knew'st what I dreamt, when thou knew'st
    when
Excesse of joy would wake me, and cam'st then,
I must confesse, it could not chuse but bee
Prophane, to thinke thee any thing but thee.

Comming and staying show'd thee, thee,
But rising makes me doubt, that now,
     Thou art not thou.
That love is weake, where feare's as strong as hee;
'Tis not all spirit, pure, and brave,
If mixture it of *Feare*, *Shame*, *Honor*, have.
Perchance as torches which must ready bee,
Men light and put out, so thou deal'st with mee,
Thou cam'st to kindle, goest to come; Then I
Will dreame that hope againe, but else would die.

A VALEDICTION: OF WEEPING

    Let me powre forth
My teares before thy face, whil'st I stay here,
For thy face coines them, and thy stampe they beare,
And by this Mintage they are something worth,
    For thus they bee
    Pregnant of thee;
Fruits of much griefe they are, emblems of more,
When a teare falls, that thou falls which it bore,
So thou and I are nothing then, when on a divers shore.

    On a round ball
A workeman that hath copies by, can lay
An Europe, Afrique, and an Asia,
And quickly make that, which was nothing, *All*:
    So doth each teare,
    Which thee doth weare,
A globe, yea world by that impression grow,
Till thy teares mixt with mine doe overflow
This world, by waters sent from thee, my heaven dissolved so.

O more than Moone,
Draw not up seas to drowne me in thy spheare,
Weepe me not dead, in thine armes, but forbeare
To teach the sea, what it may doe too soone;
Let not the winde
Example finde,
To doe me more harme, than it purposeth;
Since thou and I sigh one anothers breath,
Who e'r sighes most, is cruellest, and hastes the others death.

LOVES ALCHYMIE

Some that have deeper digg'd loves Myne than I,
Say, where his centrique happinesse doth lie:
I have lov'd, and got, and told,
But should I love, get, tell, till I were old,
I should not finde that hidden mysterie;
Oh, 'tis imposture all:
And as no chymique yet th'Elixar got,
But glorifies his pregnant pot,
If by the way to him befall
Some odoriferous thing, or medicinall,
So, lovers dreame a rich and long delight,
But get a winter-seeming summers night.

Our ease, our thrift, our honor, and our day,
Shall we, for this vaine Bubles shadow pay?
Ends love in this, that my man,
Can be as happy'as I can; If he can
Endure the short scorne of a Bridegroomes play?
That loving wretch that sweares,
'Tis not the bodies marry, but the mindes,
Which he in her Angelique findes,

Would sweare as justly, that he heares,
In that dayes rude hoarse minstralsey, the spheares.
    Hope not for minde in women; at their best
    Sweetnesse and wit, they'are but *Mummy*, possest.

THE FLEA

Marke but this flea, and marke in this,
How little that which thou deny'st me is;
It suck'd me first, and now sucks thee,
And in this flea, our two bloods mingled bee;
Thou know'st that this cannot be said
A sinne, nor shame, nor losse of maidenhead,
    Yet this enjoyes before it wooe,
    And pamper'd swells with one blood made of two,
    And this, alas, is more than wee would doe.

Oh stay, three lives in one flea spare,
Where wee almost, yea more than maryed are.
This flea is you and I, and this
Our mariage bed, and mariage temple is;
Though parents grudge, and you, w'are met,
And cloysterd in these living walls of Jet.
    Though use make you apt to kill mee,
    Let not to that, selfe murder added bee,
    And sacrilege, three sinnes in killing three.

Cruell and sodaine, hast thou since
Purpled thy naile, in blood of innocence?
Wherein could this flea guilty bee,
Except in that drop which it suckt from thee?
Yet thou triumph'st, and saist that thou
Find'st not thy selfe, nor mee the weaker now;
    'Tis true, then learne how false, feares bee;
    Just so much honor, when thou yeeld'st to mee,
    Will wast, as this flea's death tooke life from thee.

THE CURSE

Who ever guesses, thinks, or dreames he knowes
Who is my mistris, wither by this curse;
  His only, and only his purse
  May some dull heart to love dispose,
And shee yeeld then to all that are his foes;
 May he be scorn'd by one, whom all else scorne,
 Forsweare to others, what to her he'hath sworne,
 With feare of missing, shame of getting, torne:

Madnesse his sorrow, gout his cramp, may hee
Make, by but thinking, who hath made him such:
  And may he feele no touch
  Of conscience, but of fame, and bee
Anguish'd, not that'twas sinne, but that'twas shee:
 In early and long scarcenesse may he rot,
 For land which had been his, if he had not
 Himselfe incestuously an heire begot:

May he dreame Treason, and beleeve, that hee
Meant to performe it, and confesse, and die,
  And no record tell why:
  His sonnes, which none of his may bee,
Inherite nothing but his infamie:
 Or may he so long Parasites have fed,
 That he would faine be theirs, whom he hath bred,
 And at the last be circumcis'd for bread:

The venom of all stepdames, gamsters gall,
What Tyrans, and their subjects interwish,
  What Plants, Myne, Beasts, Foule, Fish,
  Can contribute, all ill which all
Prophets, or Poets spake; And all which shall

Be annex'd in schedules unto this by mee,
Fall on that man; For if it be a shee
Nature beforehand hath out-cursed mee.

A NOCTURNALL UPON S. LUCIES DAY,
BEING THE SHORTEST DAY[1]

Tis the yeares midnight, and it is the dayes,
Lucies, who scarce seaven houres herself unmaskes,
The Sunne is spent, and now his flasks
Send forth light squibs, no constant rayes;
The worlds whole sap is sunke:
The generall balme th'hydroptique earth hath drunk,
Whither, as to the beds-feet, life is shrunke,
Dead and enterr'd; yet all these seeme to laugh,
Compar'd with mee, who am their Epitaph.

Study me then, you who shall lovers bee
At the next world, that is, at the next Spring:
For I am every dead thing,
In whom love wrought new Alchimie.
For his art did expresse
A quintessence even from nothingnesse,
From dull privations, and leane emptinesse
He ruin'd mee, and I am re-begot
Of absence, darknesse, death; things which are not.

All others, from all things, draw all that's good,
Life, soule, forme, spirit, whence they beeing have;
I, by loves limbecke, am the grave
Of all, that's nothing. Oft a flood
Have wee two wept, and so

---

1. 13 December (12 December O.S., according to the old calendar, 22
December N.S.), the day of the Winter Solstice, when the sun enters
the sign of Capricorn (*v.* l. 39).

Drownd the whole world, us two; oft did we grow
To be two Chaosses, when we did show
Care to ought else; and often absences
Withdrew our soules, and made us carcasses.

But I am by her death, (which word wrongs her)
Of the first nothing, the Elixer grown;
   Were I a man, that I were one,
   I need must know; I should preferre,
     If I were any beast,
Some ends, some means; Yea plants, yea stones detest,
And love; All, all some properties invest;
If I an ordinary nothing were,
As shadow, a light, and body must be here.

But I am None; nor will my Sunne renew.
You lovers, for whose sake, the lesser Sunne
   At this time to the Goat is runne
   To fetch new lust, and give it you,
     Enjoy your summer all;
Since shee enjoyes her long nights festivall,
Let mee prepare towards her, and let mee call
This houre her Vigill, and her Eve, since this
Both the yeares, and the dayes deep midnight is.

WITCHCRAFT BY A PICTURE

I fixe mine eye on thine, and there
   Pitty my picture burning in thine eye,
My picture drown'd in a transparent teare,
   When I looke lower I espie;

Hadst thou the wicked skill
By pictures made and mard, to kill,
How many wayes mightst thou performe thy will?

But now I have drunke thy sweet salt teares,
    And though thou poure more I'll depart;
My picture vanish'd, vanish feares,
    That I can be endamag'd by that art:
        Though thou retaine of mee
One picture more, yet that will bee,
Being in thine owne heart, from all malice free.

THE APPARITION

When by thy scorne, O murdresse, I am dead,
And that thou thinkst thee free
From all solicitation from mee,
Then shall my ghost come to thy bed,
And thee, fain'd vestall, in worse armes shall see;
Then thy sicke taper will begin to winke,
And he, whose thou art then, being tyr'd before,
Will, if thou stirre, or pinch to wake him, thinke
        Thou call'st for more,
And in false sleepe will from thee shrinke,
And then poore Aspen wretch, neglected thou
Bath'd in a cold quicksilver sweat wilt lye
        A veryer ghost than I;
What I will say, I will not tell thee now,
Lest that preserve thee'; and since my love is spent,
I'had rather thou shouldst painfully repent,
Than by my threatnings rest still innocent.

THE BROKEN HEART

He is starke mad, who ever sayes,
   That he hath beene in love an houre,
Yet not that love so soone decayes,
   But that it can tenne in lesse space devour;
Who will beleeve mee, if I sweare
That I have had the plague a yeare?
   Who would not laugh at mee, if I should say,
   I saw a flaske of *powder burne a day?*

Ah, what a trifle is a heart,
   If once into loves hands it come!
All other griefes allow a part
   To other griefes, and aske themselves but some;
They come to us, but us Love draws,
Hee swallows us, and never chawes:
   By him, as by chain'd shot, whole rankes doe dye,
   He is the tyran Pike, our hearts the Frye.

If 'twere not so, what did become
   Of my heart, when I first saw thee?
I brought a heart into the roome,
   But from the roome, I carried none with mee:
If it had gone to thee, I know
Mine would have taught thine heart to show
   More pitty unto mee: but Love, alas,
   At one first blow did shiver it as glasse.

Yet nothing can to nothing fall,
   Nor any place be empty quite,
Therefore I thinke my breast hath all
   Those peeces still, though they be not unite;

And now as broken glasses show
A hundred lesser faces, so
    My ragges of heart can like, wish, and adore,
    But after one such love, can love no more.

A VALEDICTION: FORBIDDING MOURNING

As virtuous men passe mildly away,
    And whisper to their soules, to goe,
Whilst some of their sad friends doe say,
    The breath goes now, and some say, no:

So let us melt, and make no noise,
    No teare-floods, nor sigh-tempests move,
T'were prophanation of our joyes
    To tell the layetie our love.

Moving of th'earth brings harmes and feares,
    Men reckon what it did and meant,
But trepidation of the spheares,[1]
    Though greater farre, is innocent.

Dull sublunary lovers love
    (Whose soule is sense) cannot admit
Absence, because it doth remove
    Those things which elemented it.

But we by a love, so much refin'd,
    That our selves know not what it is,
Inter-assured of the mind,
    Care lesse, eyes, lips, and hands to misse.

---

1. The precession of the equinoxes was caused, according to Ptolemaic astronomy, by the swaying motion or 'trepidation' of the ninth, or Crystalline sphere.

Our two soules therefore, which are one,
  Though I must goe, endure not yet
A breach, but an expansion,
  Like gold to ayery thinnesse beate.

If they be two, they are two so
  As stiffe twin compasses are two,
Thy soule the fixt foot, makes no show
  To move, but doth, if the'other doe.

And though it in the center sit,
  Yet when the other far doth rome,
It leanes, and hearkens after it,
  And growes erect, as that comes home.

Such wilt thou be to mee, who must
  Like th'other foot, obliquely runne;
Thy firmnes drawes my circle just,
  And makes me end, where I begunne.

THE EXTASIE

Where, like a pillow on a bed,
  A Pregnant banke swel'd up, to rest
The violets reclining head,
  Sat we two, one anothers best.
Our hands were firmely cimented
  With a fast balme, which thence did spring,
Our eye-beames twisted, and did thred
  Our eyes, upon one double string;
So to'entergraft our hands, as yet
  Was all the meanes to make us one,
And pictures in our eyes to get
  Was all our propagation.

As 'twixt two equall Armies, Fate
   Suspends uncertaine victorie,
Our soules, (which to advance their state,
   Were gone out,) hung 'twixt her, and mee.
And whil'st our soules negotiate there,
   Wee like sepulchrall statues lay;
All day, the same our postures were,
   And wee said nothing, all the day.
If any, so by love refin'd,
   That he soules language understood,
And by good love were growen all minde,
   Within convenient distance stood,
He (though he knew not which soul spake,
   Because both meant, both spake the same)
Might thence a new concoction take,
   And part farre purer than he came.
This Extasie doth unperplex
   (We said) and tell us what we love,
Wee see by this, it was not sexe,
   Wee see, we saw not what did move:
But as all severall soules containe
   Mixture of things, they know not what,
Love, these mixt soules, doth mixe againe,
   And makes both one, each this and that.
A single violet transplant,
   The strength, the colour, and the size,
(All which before was poore, and scant,)
   Redoubles still, and multiplies.
When love, with one another so
   Interinanimates two soules,
That abler soule, which thence doth flow,
   Defects of lonelinesse controules.
Wee then, who are this new soule, know,
   Of what we are compos'd, and made,

For, th'Atomies of which we grow,
    Are soules, whom no change can invade.
But O alas, so long, so farre
    Our bodies why doe wee forbeare?
They are ours, though they are not wee, Wee are
    The intelligences, they the spheares.
We owe them thankes, because they thus,
    Did us, to us, at first convay,
Yeelded their forces, sense, to us,
    Nor are drosse to us, but allay.
On man heavens influence workes not so,
    But that it first imprints the ayre,
Soe soule into the soule may flow,
    Though it to body first repaire.
As our blood labours to beget
    Spirits, as like soules as it can,
Because such fingers need to knit
    That subtile knot, which makes us man:
So must pure lovers soules descend
    T'affections, and to faculties,
Which sense may reach and apprehend,
    Else a great Prince in prison lies.
To'our bodies turne wee then, that so
    Weake men on love reveal'd may looke;
Loves mysteries in soules doe grow,
    But yet the body is his booke.
And if some lover, such as wee,
    Have heard this dialogue of one,
Let him still marke us, he shall see
    Small change, when we'are to bodies gone.

LOVES DEITIE

I long to talke with some old lovers ghost,
   Who dyed before the god of Love was borne:
I cannot thinke that hee, who then lov'd most,
   Sunke so low, as to love one which did scorne.
But since this god produc'd a destinie,
And that vice-nature, custome, lets it be;
   I must love her, that loves not mee.

Sure, they which made him god, meant not so much,
   Nor he, in his young godhead practis'd it.
But when an even flame two hearts did touch,
   His office was indulgently to fit.
Actives to passives. Correspondencie
Only his subject was; It cannot bee
   Love, till I love her, that loves mee.

But every moderne god will now extend
   His vast prerogative, as far as Jove.
To rage, to lust, to write to, to commend,
   All is the purlewe of the God of Love.
Oh were wee wak'ned by this Tyrannie
To ungod this child againe, it could not bee
   I should love her, who loves not mee.

Rebell and Atheist too, why murmure I,
   As though I felt the worst that love could doe?
Love might make me leave loving, or might trie
   A deeper plague, to make her love mee too,
Which, since she loves before, I'am loth to see;
Falshood is worse than hate; and that must bee,
   If shee whom I love, should love mee.

THE WILL

Before I sigh my last gaspe, let me breath,
Great love, some Legacies; Here I bequeath
Mine eyes to *Argus*, if mine eyes can see,
If they be blinde, then Love, I give them thee;
My tongue to Fame; to'Embassadours mine eares;
   To women or the sea, my teares.
Thou, Love, hast taught mee heretofore
By making mee serve her who'had twenty more,
That I should give to none, but such, as had too much
    before.

My constancie I to the planets give;
My truth to them, who at the Court doe live;
Mine ingenuity and opennesse,
To Jesuites; to Buffones my pensivenesse;
My silence to'any, who abroad hath beene;
   My mony to a Capuchin.
Thou Love taught'st me, by appointing mee
To love there, where no love receiv'd can be,
Onely to give to such as have an incapacitie.

My faith I give to Roman Catholiques;
All my good works unto the Schismaticks
Of Amsterdam: my best civility
And Courtship, to an Universitie;
My modesty I give to souldiers bare;
   My patience let gamesters share.
Thou Love taughtst mee, by making mee
Love her that holds my love disparity,
Onely to give to those that count my gifts indignity.

I give my reputation to those
Which were my friends; Mine industrie to foes;
To Schoolemen I bequeath my doubtfulnesse;
My sicknesse to Physitians, or excesse;
To Nature, all that I in Ryme have writ;
    And to my company my wit.
Thou Love, by making mee adore
Her, who begot this love in mee before,
Taughtst me to make, as though I gave, when I did but
    restore.

To him for whom the passing bell next tolls,
I give my physick bookes; my writen rowles
Of Morall counsels, I to Bedlam give;
My brazen medals, unto them which live
In want of bread; To them which passe among
    All forrainers, mine English tongue.
Thou, Love, by making mee love one
Who thinkes her friendship a fit portion
For yonger lovers, dost my gifts thus disproportion.

Therefore I'll give no more; But I'll undoe
The world by dying; because love dies too.
Then all your beauties will bee no more worth
Than gold in Mines, where none doth draw it forth;
And all your graces no more use shall have
    Than a Sun dyall in a grave.
Thou Love taughtst mee, by making mee
Love her, who doth neglect both mee and thee,
To'invent, and practise this one way, to'annihilate all
    three.

THE FUNERALL[1]

Who ever comes to shroud me, do not harme
      Nor question much
That subtile wreath of haire, which crowns my arme;
The mystery, the signe you must not touch,
      For'tis my outward Soule,
Viceroy to that, which then to heaven being gone,
      Will leave this to controule,
And keep these limbes, her Provinces, from dissolution.

For if the sinewie thread my braine lets fall
      Through every part,
Can tye those parts, and make mee one of all;
These haires which upward grew, and strength and art
      Have from a better braine,
Can better do'it; Except she meant that I
      By this should know my pain,
As prisoners then are manacled, when they'are condemn'd
      to die.

What ere shee meant by'it, bury it with me,
      For since I am
Loves martyr, it might breed idolatrie,
If into others hands these Reliques came;
      As'twas humility
To afford to it all that a Soule can doe,
      So,'tis some bravery,
That since you would save none of mee, I bury some of
      you.

1. This and the three following poems have been wrongly associated with Magdalen Herbert and the early years of her friendship with the poet.

THE BLOSSOME

Little think'st thou, poore flower,
  Whom I have watch'd sixe or seaven dayes,
And seene thy birth, and seene what every houre
Gave to thy growth, thee to this height to raise,
And now dost laugh and triumph on this bough,
      Little think'st thou
That it will freeze anon, and that I shall
To morrow finde thee falne, or not at all.

Little think'st thou poore heart
  That labour'st yet to nestle thee,
And think'st by hovering here to get a part
In a forbidden or forbidding tree,
And hop'st her stiffenesse by long siege to bow:
      Little think'st thou,
That thou to morrow, ere that Sunne doth wake,
Must with this Sunne, and mee a journey take.

But thou which lov'st to bee
  Subtile to plague thy selfe, wilt say,
Alas, if you must goe, what's that to mee?
Here lyes my businesse, and here I will stay:
You goe to friends, whose love and meanes present
      Various content
To your eyes, eares, and tongue, and every part.
If then your body goe, what need you a heart?

Well then, stay here; but know,
  When thou hast stayd and done thy most;
A naked thinking heart, that makes no show,
Is to a woman, but a kinde of Ghost;

How shall shee know my heart; or having none,
     Know thee for one?
Practise may make her know some other part,
But take my word, shee doth not know a Heart.

  Meet mee at London, then,
    Twenty dayes hence, and thou shalt see
Mee fresher, and more fat, by being with men,
Than if I had staid still with her and thee.
For Gods sake, if you can, be you so too:
     I would give you
There, to another friend, whom wee shall finde
As glad to have my body, as my minde.

THE PRIMROSE,

BEING AT MONTGOMERY CASTLE,
UPON THE HILL, ON WHICH IT
IS SITUATE[1]

Upon this Primrose hill,
    Where, if Heav'n would distill
A shoure of raine, each severall drop might goe
To his owne primrose, and grow Manna so;
And where their forme, and their infinitie
    Make a terrestriall Galaxie,
    As the small starres doe in the skie:
I walke to finde a true Love; and I see
That'tis not a mere woman, that is shee,
But must, or more, or lesse than woman bee.

    Yet know I not, which flower
    I wish; a sixe, or foure;

---

1. Montgomery Castle, home of Magdalen, Lady Herbert, mother of the
poets, George Herbert and Edward, Lord Herbert of Cherbury.

For should my true-Love lesse than woman bee,
She were scarce any thing; and then, should she
Be more than woman, shee would get above
      All thought of sexe, and thinke to move
      My heart to study her, and not to love;
Both these were monsters; Since there must reside
Falshood in woman, I could more abide,
She were by art, than Nature falsify'd.

      Live Primrose then, and thrive
      With thy true number five;
And women, whom this flower doth represent,
With this mysterious number be content;
Ten is the farthest number; if halfe ten
      Belonge unto each woman, then
      Each woman may take halfe us men;
Or if this will not serve their turne, Since all
Numbers are odde, or even, and they fall
First into this, five, women may take us all.

THE RELIQUE

      When my grave is broke up againe
      Some second ghest to entertaine,
      (For graves have learn'd that woman-head
      To be to more than one a Bed)
        And he that digs it, spies
A bracelet of bright haire about the bone,
      Will he not let'us alone,
And thinke that there a loving couple lies,
Who thought that this device might be some way
To make their soules, at the last busie day,
Meet at this grave, and make a little stay?

If this fall in a time, or land,
Where mis-devotion doth command,
Then, he that digges us up, will bring
Us, to the Bishop, and the King,
To make us Reliques; then
Thou shalt be a Mary Magdalen, and I
A something else thereby;
All women shall adore us, and some men;
And since at such time, miracles are sought,
I would have that age by this paper taught
What miracles wee harmelesse lovers wrought.

First, we lov'd well and faithfully,
Yet knew not what wee lov'd, nor why,
Difference of sex no more wee knew,
Than our Guardian Angells doe;
Comming and going, wee
Perchance might kisse, but not between those meales;
Our hands ne'r toucht the seales,
Which nature, injur'd by late law, sets free:
These miracles wee did; but now alas,
All measure, and all language, I should passe,
Should I tell what a miracle shee was.

THE DAMPE

When I am dead, and Doctors know not why,
And my friends curiositie
Will have me cut up to survay each part,
When they shall finde your Picture in my heart,
You thinke a sodaine dampe of love
Will through all their senses move,
And worke on them as mee, and so preferre
Your murder, to the name of Massacre.

Poore victories! But if you dare be brave,
    And pleasure in your conquest have,
First kill th'enormous Gyant, your *Disdaine*,
And let th'enchantresse *Honor*, next be slaine,
    And like a Goth and Vandall rize,
    Deface Records, and Histories
Of your owne arts and triumphs over men,
And without such advantage kill me then.

For I could muster up as well as you
    My Gyants, and my Witches too,
Which are vast *Constancy*, and *Secretnesse*,
But these I neyther looke for, nor professe;
    Kill mee as Woman, let mee die
  As a meere man; doe you but try
Your passive valor, and you shall finde then,
Naked you'have odds enough of any man.

THE PROHIBITION

    Take heed of loving mee
At least remember, I forbade it thee;
Not that I shall repaire my'unthrifty wast
Of Breath and Blood, upon thy sighes, and teares,
By being to thee then what to me thou wast;
But, so great Joy, our life at once outweares,
Then, lest thy love, by my death, frustrate bee,
If thou love mee, take heed of loving mee.

    Take heed of hating mee,
Or too much triumph in the Victorie.
Not that I shall be mine owne officer,
And hate with hate againe retaliate;
But thou wilt lose the stile of conquerour,

If I, thy conquest, perish by thy hate.
Then, lest my being nothing lessen thee,
If thou hate mee, take heed of hating mee.

    Yet, love and hate mee too,
So, these extreames shall neithers office doe;
Love mee, that I may die the gentler way;
Hate mee, because thy love is too great for mee;
Or let these two, themselves, not me decay;
So shall I, live, thy Stage, not triumph bee;
Lest thou thy love and hate and mee undoe,
To let mee live, O love and hate mee too.

THE EXPIRATION

So, so, breake off this last lamenting kisse,
   Which sucks two soules, and vapors Both away,
Turne thou ghost that way, and let mee turne this,
   And let our selves benight our happiest day,
We ask'd none leave to love; nor will we owe
   Any, so cheape a death, as saying, Goe;

Goe; and if that word have not quite kil'd thee,
   Ease mee with death, by bidding mee goe too.
Oh, if it have, let my word worke on mee,
   And a just office on a murderer doe.
Except it be too late, to kill me so,
   Being doubled dead, going, and bidding, goe.

A LECTURE UPON THE SHADOW

Stand still, and I will read to thee
A Lecture, love, in Loves philosophy.
    These three houres that we have spent,
    Walking here, Two shadowes went
Along with us, which we our selves produc'd;
But, now the Sunne is just above our head,
    We doe those shadowes tread;
    And to brave clearnesse all things are reduc'd.
  So whilst our infant loves did grow,
  Disguises did, and shadowes, flow,
  From us, and our cares; but, now 'tis not so.

That love hath not attain'd the high'st degree,
Which is still diligent lest others see.

Except our loves at this noone stay,
We shall new shadowes make the other way.
    As the first were made to blinde
    Others; these which come behinde
Will worke upon our selves, and blind our eyes.
If our loves faint, and westwardly decline;
    To me thou, falsly, thine,
    And I to thee mine actions shall disguise.
  The morning shadowes weare away,
  But these grow longer all the day,
  But oh, loves day is short, if love decay.

Love is a growing, or full constant light;
And his first minute, after noone, is night.

ELEGIES

ELEGIE I

JEALOSIE

Fond woman, which would'st have thy husband die,
And yet complain'st of his great jealousie;
If swolne with poyson, hee lay in 'his last bed,
His body with a sere-barke covered,
Drawing his breath, as thick and short, as can
The nimblest crocheting Musitian,
Ready with loathsome vomiting to spue
His Soule out of one hell, into a new,
Made deafe with his poore kindreds howling cries,
Begging with few feign'd teares, great legacies,
Thou would'st not weepe, but jolly,' and frolicke bee,
As a slave, which to morrow should be free;
Yet weep'st thou, when thou seest him hungerly
Swallow his owne death, hearts-bane jealousie.
O give him many thanks, he'is courteous,
That in suspecting kindly warneth us.
Wee must not, as wee us'd, flout openly,
In scoffing ridles, his deformitie;
Nor at his boord together being satt,
With words, nor touch, scarce lookes adulterate.
Nor when he swolne, and pamper'd with great fare
Sits downe, and snorts, cag'd in his basket chaire,
Must wee usurpe his owne bed any more,
  Nor kisse and play in his house, as before.
Now I see many dangers; for that is
His realme, his castle, and his diocesse.

But if, as envious men, which would revile
Their Prince, or coyne his gold, themselves exile
Into another countrie,'and doe it there,
Wee play'in another house, what should we feare?
There we will scorne his houshold policies,
His seely plots, and pensionary spies,
As the inhabitants of Thames right side
Do Londons Major[1]; or Germans, the Popes pride.

ELEGIE II

THE ANAGRAM

Marry, and love thy *Flavia*, for, shee
Hath all things, whereby others beautious bee,
For, though her eyes be small, her mouth is great,
Though they be Ivory, yet her teeth be jeat,
Though they be dimme, yet she is light enough,
And though her harsh haire fall, her skinne is rough;
What though her cheeks be yellow, her haire's red,
Give her thine, and she hath a maydenhead.
These things are beauties elements, where these
Meet in one, that one must, as perfect, please.
If red and white and each good quality
Be in thy wench, ne'r aske where it doth lye.
In buying things perfum'd, we aske; if there
Be muske and amber in it, but not where.
Though all her parts be not in th'usuall place,
She'hath yet an Anagram of a good face.
If we might put the letters but one way,
In the leane dearth of words, what could wee say?
When by the Gamut some Musitions make
A perfect song, others will undertake,

1. *i.e.* The Lord Mayor of London. This spelling is now obsolete.

By the same Gamut chang'd, to equall it.
Things simply good, can never be unfit.
She's faire as any, if all be like her,
And if none bee, then she is singular.
All love is wonder; if wee justly doe
Account her wonderfull, why not lovely too?
Love built on beauty, soone as beauty, dies,
Chuse this face, chang'd by no deformities.
Women are all like Angels; the faire be
Like those which fell to worse; but such as thee,
Like to good Angels, nothing can impaire:
'Tis lesse griefe to be foule, than to'have beene faire.
For one nights revels, silke and gold we chuse,
But, in long journeyes, cloth, and leather use.
Beauty is barren oft; best husbands say,
There is best land, where there is foulest way.
Oh what a soveraigne Plaister will shee bee,
If thy past sinnes have taught thee jealousie!
Here needs no spies, nor eunuches; her commit
Safe to thy foes; yea, to a Marmosit.[1]
When Belgiaes citties, the round countries drowne,
That durty foulenesse guards, and armes the towne:
So doth her face guard her; and so, for thee,
Which, forc'd by businesse, absent oft must bee,
Shee, whose face, like clouds, turnes the day to night,
Who, mightier than the sea, makes Moores seem white,
Who, though seaven yeares, she in the Stews had laid,
A Nunnery durst receive, and thinke a maid,
And though in childbeds labour she did lie,
Midwifes would sweare,'twere but a tympanie,
Whom, if shee accuse her selfe, I credit lesse
Than witches, which impossibles confesse,

1. Applied, as here, to a man 'marmosit' is a term of contempt, meaning a
    wanton, apish sort of gallant or minion.

Whom Dildoes, Bedstaves, and her Velvet Glasse
Would be as loath to touch as Joseph was:
One like none, and lik'd of none, fittest were,
For, things in fashion every man will weare.

ELEGIE III

CHANGE

Although thy hand and faith, and good workes too,
Have seal'd thy love which nothing should undoe,
Yea though thou fall backe, that apostasie
Confirme thy love; yet much, much I feare thee.
Women are like the Arts, forc'd unto none,
Open to'all searchers, unpriz'd, if unknowne.
If I have caught a bird, and let him flie,
Another fouler using these meanes, as I,
May catch the same bird; and, as these things bee,
Women are made for men, not him, nor mee.
Foxes and goats; all beasts change when they please,
Shall women, more hot, wily, wild than these,
Be bound to one man, and did Nature then
Idly make them apter to'endure than men?
They'are our clogges, not their owne; if a man bee
Chain'd to a galley, yet the galley'is free;
Who hath a plow-land, casts all his seed corne there,
And yet allowes his ground more corne should beare;
Though Danuby into the sea must flow,
The sea receives the Rhene, Volga, and Po.
By nature, which gave it, this liberty
Thou lov'st, but Oh! canst thou love it and mee?
Likenesse glues love: and if that thou so doe,
To make us like and love, must I change too?

More than thy hate, I hate'it, rather let mee
Allow her change, than change as oft as shee,
And soe not teach, but force my'opinion
To love not any one, nor every one.
To live in one land, is captivitie,
To runne all countries, a wild roguery;
Waters stincke soone, if in one place they bide,
And in the vast sea are more putrifi'd:
But when they kisse one banke, and leaving this
Never looke backe, but the next banke doe kisse,
Then are they purest; Change'is the nursery
Of musicke, joy, life, and eternity.

ELEGIE IV

THE PERFUME

Once, and but once found in thy company,
All thy suppos'd escapes[1] are laid on mee;
And as a thiefe at barre, is question'd there
By all the men, that have beene rob'd that yeare,
So am I, (by this traiterous meanes surpriz'd)
By thy Hydroptique father catechiz'd.
Though he had wont to search with glazed eyes,
As though he came to kill a Cockatrice,
Though hee hath oft sworne, that hee would remove
Thy beauties beautie, and food of our love,
Hope of his goods, if I with thee were seene,
Yet close and secret, as our soules, we'have beene.
Though thy immortall mother which doth lye
Still buried in her bed, yet will not dye,
Takes this advantage to sleepe out day-light,
And watch thy entries, and returnes all night,

---

1. In the now obsolete sense of 'escapades'.

And, when she takes thy hand, and would seeme kind,
Doth search what rings, and armelets she can finde,
And kissing notes the colour of thy face,
And fearing least thou'art swolne, doth thee embrace;
To trie if thou long, doth name strange meates,
And notes thy palenesse, blushing, sighs, and sweats;
And politiquely will to thee confesse
The sinnes of her owne youths ranke lustinesse;
Yet love these Sorceries did remove, and move
Thee to gull thine owne mother for my love.
Thy little brethren, which like Faiery Sprights
Oft skipt into our chamber, those sweet nights,
And kist, and ingled on thy fathers knee,
Were brib'd next day, to tell what they did see:
The grim eight-foot-high iron-bound serving-man,
That oft names God in oathes, and onely then,
He that to barre the first gate, doth as wide
As the great Rhodian Colossus stride,
Which, if in hell no other paines there were,
Makes mee feare hell, because he must be there:
Though by thy father he were hir'd to this,
Could never witnesse any touch or kisse.
But Oh, too common ill, I brought with mee
That, which betray'd mee to my enemie:
A loud perfume, which at my entrance cryed
Even at thy fathers nose, so were wee spied.
When, like a tyran King, that in his bed
Smelt gunpowder, the pale wretch shivered.
Had it beene some bad smell, he would have thought
That his owne feet, or breath, that smell had wrought.
But as wee in our Ile emprisoned,
Where cattell onely,'and diverse dogs are bred,
The pretious Unicornes, strange monsters call,
So thought he good, strange, that had none at all.

I taught my silkes, their whistling to forbeare,
Even my opprest shoes, dumbe and speechlesse were,
Onely, thou bitter sweet, whom I had laid
Next mee, mee traiterously hast betraid,
And unsuspected hast invisibly
At once fled unto him, and staid with mee.
Base excrement of earth, which dost confound
Sense, from distinguishing the sicke from sound;
By thee the seely Amorous sucks his death
By drawing in a leprous harlots breath;
By thee, the greatest staine to mans estate
Falls on us, to be call'd effeminate;
Though you be much lov'd in the Princes hall,
There, things that seeme, exceed substantiall.
Gods, when yee fum'd on altars, were pleas'd well,
Because you'were burnt, not that they lik'd your smell;
You'are loathsome all, being taken simply alone,
Shall wee love ill things joyn'd, and hate each one?
If you were good, your good doth soone decay;
And you are rare, that takes the good away.
All my perfumes, I give most willingly
To'embalme thy fathers corse; What? will hee die?

ELEGIE V

HIS PICTURE

Here take my Picture; though I bid farewell,
Thine, in my heart, where my soule dwels, shall dwell.
'Tis like me now, but I dead, 'twill be more
When wee are shadowes both, than'twas before.
When weather-beaten I come backe; my hand,
Perhaps with rude oares torne, or Sun beams tann'd,

My face and brest of hairecloth, and my head
With cares rash sodaine stormes, being o'rspread,
My body'a sack of bones, broken within,
And powders blew staines scatter'd on my skinne;
If rivall fooles taxe thee to'have lov'd a man,
So foule, and coarse, as, Oh, I may seeme then,
This shall say what I was: and thou shalt say,
Doe his hurts reach mee? doth my worth decay?
Or doe they reach his judging minde, that hee
Should now love lesse, what hee did love to see?
That which in him was faire and delicate,
Was but the milke, which in loves childish state
Did nurse it: who now is growne strong enough
To feed on that, which to disus'd tasts seemes tough.

ELEGIE VII

Natures lay Ideot, I taught thee to love,
And in that sophistrie, Oh, thou dost prove
Too subtile: Foole, thou didst not understand
The mystique language of the eye nor hand:
Nor couldst thou judge the difference of the aire
Of sighes, and say, this lies, this sounds despaire:
Nor by the'eyes water call a maladie
Desperately hot, or changing feaverously.
I had not taught thee then, the Alphabet
Of flowers, how they devisefully being set
And bound up, might with speechlesse secrecie
Deliver errands mutely, and mutually.
Remember since all thy words us'd to bee
To every suitor; *Ay, if my friends agree*;
Since, houshold charmes, thy husbands name to teach,
Were all the love trickes, that thy wit could reach;

And since, an houres discourse could scarce have made
One answer in thee, and that ill arraid
In broken proverbs, and torne sentences.
Thou art not by so many duties his,
That from the worlds Common having sever'd thee,
Inlaid[1] thee, neither to be seene, nor see,
As mine: who have with amorous delicacies
Refin'd thee'into a blis-full Paradise.
Thy graces and good words my creatures bee;
I planted knowledge and lifes tree in thee,
Which Oh, shall strangers taste? Must I alas
Frame and enamell Plate, and drinke in Glasse?
Chafe waxe for others seales? breake a colts force
And leave him then, beeing made a ready horse?

ELEGIE IX[2]

THE AUTUMNALL

No *Spring*, nor *Summer* Beauty hath such grace,
    As I have seen in one *Autumnall* face.
Yong *Beauties* force our love, and that's a *Rape*,
    This doth but *counsaile*, yet you cannot scape.
If t'were a *shame* to love, here t'were no *shame*,
    Affection here takes *Reverences* name.
Were her first yeares the *Golden Age*; That's true,
    But now she's *gold* oft tried, and ever new.
That was her torrid and inflaming time,
    This is her tolerable *Tropique clyme*.
Fairee yes, who askes more heate than comes from hence,
    He in a fever wishes pestilence.

1. *i.e.* Laid up, or away, in a place of concealment. A rare usage.
2. Addressed to Magdalen Herbert, *c.* 1607–8, before her second marriage to Sir John Danvers.

Call not these wrinkles, *graves*; If *graves* they were,
   They were *Loves graves*; for else he is no where.
Yet lies not Love *dead* here, but here doth sit
   Vow'd to this trench, like an *Anachorit*.
And here, till hers, which must be his *death*, come,
   He doth not digge a *Grave*, but build a *Tombe*.
Here dwells he, though he sojourne ev'ry where,
   In *Progresse*, yet his standing house is here.
Here, where still *Evening* is; not *noone*, nor *night*;
   Where no *voluptuousnesse*, yet all *delight*.
In all her words, unto all hearers fit,
   You may at *Revels*, you at *Counsaile*, sit.
This is loves timber, youth his under-wood;
   There he, as wine in *June*, enrages blood,
Which then comes seasonabliest, when our tast
   And appetite to other things, is past.
Xerxes strange *Lydian* love, the *Platane* tree,
   Was lov'd for age, none being so large as shee,
Or else because, being yong, nature did blesse
   Her youth with ages glory, *Barrennesse*.
If we love things long sought, *Age* is a thing
   Which we are fifty yeares in compassing.
If transitory things, which soone decay,
   Age must be lovelyest at the latest day.
But name not *Winter-faces*, whose skin's slacke;
   Lanke, as an unthrifts purse; but a soules sacke;
Whose *Eyes* seeke light within, for all here's shade;
   Whose *mouthes* are holes, rather worne out, than made;
Whose every tooth to a severall place is gone,
   To vexe their souls at *Resurrection*;
Name not these living *Deaths-heads* unto mee,
   For these, not *Ancient*, but *Antique* be.
I hate extreames; yet I had rather stay
   With *Tombs*, than *Cradles*, to weare out a day.

Since such loves naturall lation¹ is, may still
  My love descend, and journey downe the hill,
Not panting after growing beauties, so,
    I shall ebbe out with them, who home-ward goe.

ELEGIE X

THE DREAME²

Image of her whom I love, more than she,
  Whose faire impression in my faithfull heart,
Makes mee her *Medall*, and makes her love mee,
  As Kings do coynes, to which their stamps impart
The value: goe, and take my heart from hence,
  Which now is growne too great and good for me:
Honours oppresse weake spirits, and our sense
  Strong objects dull; the more, the lesse wee see.

When you are gone, and *Reason* gone with you,
  Then *Fantasie* is Queene and Soule, and all;
She can present joyes meaner than you do;
  Convenient, and more proportionall.
So, if I dreame I have you, I have you,
  For, all our joyes are but fantasticall.
And so I scape the paine, for paine is true;
  And sleepe which locks up sense, doth lock out all.

After a such fruition I shall wake,
  And, but the waking, nothing shall repent;
And shall to love more thankfull Sonnets make,
  Than if more *honour*, *teares*, and *paines* were spent.

1. A rare astronomical term, meaning 'local-motion from one place to another'.
2. In one MS copy this poem is more appropriately entitled: PICTURE.

But dearest heart, and dearer image stay;
   Alas, true joyes at best are *dreame* enough;
Though you stay here you passe too fast away:
   For even at first lifes *Taper* is a snuffe

Fill'd with her love, may I be rather grown
Mad with much *heart*, than *ideott* with none.

ELEGIE XII

HIS PARTING FROM HER

Since she must go, and I must mourn, come Night,
Environ me with darkness, whilst I write:
Shadow that hell unto me, which alone
I am to suffer when my Love is gone.
Alas the darkest Magick cannot do it,
Thou and greate Hell to boot are shadows to it.
Should *Cinthia* quit thee, *Venus*, and each starre,
It would not forme one thought dark as mine are.
I could lend thee obscureness now, and say,
Out of my self, There should be no more Day,
Such is already my felt want of sight,
Did not the fires within me force a light.
Oh Love, that fire and darkness should be mixt,
Or to thy Triumphs soe strange torments fixt!
Is't because thou thy self art blind, that wee
Thy Martyrs must no more each other see?
Or tak'st thou pride to break us on the wheel,
And view old Chaos in the Pains we feel?
Or have we left undone some mutual Rite,
Through holy fear, that merits thy despight?
No, no. The falt was mine, impute it to me.
Or rather to conspiring destinie,

Which (since I lov'd for forme before) decreed,
That I should suffer when I lov'd indeed:
And therefore now, sooner than I can say,
I saw the golden fruit, 'tis rapt away.
Or as I had watcht one drop in a vast stream,
And I left wealthy only in a dream.
Yet Love, thou'rt blinder than thy self in this,
To vex my Dove-like friend for my amiss:
And, where my own sad truth may expiate
Thy wrath, to make her fortune run my fate:
So blinded Justice doth, when Favorites fall,
Strike them, their house, their friends, their followers all.
Was't not enough that thou didst dart thy fires
Into our blouds, inflaming our desires,
And made'st us sigh and glow, and pant, and burn,
And then thy self into our flame did'st turn?
Was't not enough, that thou didst hazard us
To paths in love so dark, so dangerous:
And those so ambush'd round with houshold spies,
And over all, thy husbands towring eyes
That flam'd with oylie sweat of jealousie:
Yet went we not still on with Constancie?
Have we not kept our guards, like spie on spie?
Had correspondence whilst the foe stood by?
Stoln (more to sweeten them) our many blisses
Of meetings, conference, embracements, kisses?
Shadow'd with negligence our most respects?
Varied our language through all dialects,
Of becks, winks, looks, and often under-boards
Spoak dialogues with our feet far from our words?
Have we prov'd all these secrets of our Art,
Yea, thy pale inwards, and thy panting heart?
And, after all this passed Purgatory,
Must sad divorce make us the vulgar story?

JD–6

First let our eyes be rivited quite through
Our turning brains, and both our lips grow to:
Let our armes clasp like Ivy, and our fear
Freese us together, that we may stick here,
Till Fortune, that would rive us, with the deed,
Strain her eyes open, and it make them bleed.
For Love it cannot be, whom hitherto
I have accus'd, should such a mischief doe.
Oh Fortune, thou'rt not worth my least exclame,
And plague enough thou hast in thine own shame.
Do thy great worst, my friend and I have armes,
Though not against thy strokes, against thy harmes
Rend us in sunder, thou canst not divide
Our bodies so, but that our souls are ty'd,
And we can love by letters still and gifts,
And thoughts and dreams; Love never wanteth shifts.
I will not look upon the quickening Sun,
But straight her beauty to my sense shall run;
The ayre shall note her soft, the fire most pure;
Water suggest her clear, and the earth sure.
Time shall not lose our passages; the Spring
How fresh our love was in the beginning;
The Summer how it ripened in the eare;
And Autumn, what our golden harvests were.
The Winter I'll not think on to spite thee,
But count it a lost season, so shall shee.
And dearest Friend, since we must part, drown night
With hope of Day, burthens well born are light.
Though cold and darkness longer hang somewhere,
Yet *Phoebus* equally lights all the Sphere.
And what he cannot in like Portions pay,
The world enjoyes in Mass, and so we may.
Be then ever your self, and let no woe
Win on your health, your youth, your beauty: so

Declare your self base fortunes Enemy,
No less by your contempt than constancy:
That I may grow enamoured on your mind,
When my own thoughts I there reflected find.
For this to th'comfort of my Dear I vow,
My Deeds shall still be what my words are now;
The Poles shall move to teach me ere I start;
And when I change my Love, I'll change my heart;
Nay, if I wax but cold in my desire,
Think, heaven hath motion lost, and the world, fire:
Much more I could, but many words have made
That, oft, suspected which men would perswade;
Take therefore all in this: I love so true,
As I will never look for less in you.

ELEGIE XVI

ON HIS MISTRIS

By our first strange and fatall interview,
By all desires which thereof did ensue,
By our long starving hopes, by that remorse
Which my words masculine perswasive force
Begot in thee, and by the memory
Of hurts, which spies and rivals threatned me,
I calmly beg: But by thy fathers wrath,
By all paines, which want and divorcement hath,
I conjure thee, and all the oathes which I
And thou have sworne to seale joynt constancy,
Here I unsweare, and overswear them thus,
Thou shalt not love by wayes so dangerous.
Temper, ô faire Love, loves impetuous rage,
Be my true Mistris still, not my faign'd Page;

I'll goe, and, by thy kinde leave, leave behinde
Thee, onely worthy to nurse in my minde,
Thirst to come backe; ô if thou die before,
My soule from other lands to thee shall soare.
Thy (else Almighty) beautie cannot move
Rage from the Seas, nor thy love teach them love,
Nor tame wilde Boreas harshnesse; Thou hast reade
How roughly hee in peeces shivered
Faire Orithea, whom he swore he lov'd.
Fall ill or good, 'tis madnesse to have prov'd
Dangers unurg'd; Feed on this flattery,
That absent Lovers one in th'other be.
Dissemble nothing, not a boy, nor change
Thy bodies habite, nor mindes; bee not strange
To thy selfe onely; All will spie in thy face
A blushing womanly discovering grace;
Richly cloath'd Apes, are call'd Apes, and as soone
Ecclips'd as bright we call the Moone the Moone.
Men of France, changeable Camelions,
Spittles of diseases, shops of fashions,
Loves fuellers, and the rightest company
Of Players, which upon the worlds stage be,
Will quickly know thee, and no lesse, alas!
Th'indifferent Italian, as we passe
His warme land, well content to thinke thee Page,
Will hunt thee with such lust, and hideous rage,
As *Lots* faire guests were vext. But none of these
Nor spungy hydroptique Dutch shall thee displease,
If thou stay here. O stay here, for thee
England is onely a worthy Gallerie,
To walke in expectation, till from thence
Our greatest King call thee to his presence.
When I am gone, dreame me some happinesse,
Nor let thy lookes our long hid love confesse,

Nor praise, nor dispraise me, nor blesse nor curse
Openly loves force, nor in bed fright thy Nurse
With midnights startings, crying out, oh, oh
Nurse, ô my love is slaine, I saw him goe
O'r the white Alpes alone; I saw him I,
Assail'd, fight, taken, stabb'd, bleed, fall, and die.
Augure me better chance, except dread *Jove*
Thinke it enough for me to'have had thy love.

ELEGIE XVIII

LOVES PROGRESS

Who ever loves, if he do not propose
The right true end of love, he's one that goes
To sea for nothing but to make him sick:
Love is a bear-whelp born, if we o're lick
Our love, and force it new strange shapes to take,
We erre, and of a lump a monster make.
Were not a Calf a monster that were grown
Face'd like a man, though better than his own?
Perfection is in unitie: preferr
One woman first, and then one thing in her.
I, when I value gold, may think upon
The ductilness, the application,
The wholsomness, the ingenuitie,
From rust, from soil, from fire ever free:
But if I love it, 'tis because 'tis made
By our new nature (Use) the soul of trade.
    All these in women we might think upon
(If women had them) and yet love but one.
Can men more injure women than to say
They love them for that, by which they're not they?

Makes virtue woman? must I cool my bloud
Till I both be, and find one wise and good?
May barren Angels love so. But if we
Make love to woman; virtue is not she:
As beauty'is not nor wealth: He that strayes thus
From her to hers, is more adulterous,
Than if he took her maid. Search every sphear
And firmament, our *Cupid* is not there:
He's an infernal god and under ground,
With *Pluto* dwells, where gold and fire abound:
Men to such Gods, their sacrificing Coles
Did not in Altars lay, but pits and holes.
Although we see Celestial bodies move
Above the earth, the earth we Till and love:
So we her ayres contemplate, words and heart,
And virtues; but we love the Centrique part.

   Nor is the soul more worthy, or more fit
For love, than this, as infinite as it.
But in attaining this desired place
How much they erre; that set out at the face?
The hair a Forest is of Ambushes,
Of springes, snares, fetters and manacles:
The brow becalms us when 'tis smooth and plain,
And when 'tis wrinckled, shipwracks us again.
Smooth, 'tis a Paradice, where we would have
Immortal stay, and wrinkled 'tis our grave.
The Nose (like to the first Meridian) runs
Not 'twixt an East and West, but 'twixt two suns;
It leaves a Cheek, a rosie Hemisphere
On either side, and then directs us where
Upon the Islands fortunate we fall,
(Not faynte *Canaries*, but *Ambrosiall*)
Her swelling lips; To which when wee are come,
We anchor there, and think our selves at home,

For they seem all: there Syrens songs, and there
Wise Delphick Oracles do fill the ear;
There in a Creek where chosen pearls do swell,
The Remora, her cleaving tongue doth dwell.
These, and the glorious Promontory, her Chin
Ore past; and the streight *Hellespont* betweene
The *Sestos* and *Abydos* of her breasts,
(Not of two Lovers, but two Loves the neasts)
Succeeds a boundless sea, but yet thine eye
Some Island moles may scattered there descry;
And Sailing towards her *India*, in that way
Shall at her fair Atlantick Navell stay;
Though thence the Current be thy Pilot made,
Yet ere thou be where thou wouldst be embay'd,
Thou shalt upon another Forest set,
Where many Shipwrack, and no further get.
When thou art there, consider what this chace
Mispent by thy beginning at the face.

    Rather set out below; practice my Art,
Some Symetry the foot hath with that part
Which thou dost seek, and is thy Map for that
Lovely enough to stop, but not stay at:
Least subject to disguise and change it is;
Men say the Devil never can change his.
It is the Emblem that hath figured
Firmness; 'tis the first part that comes to bed.
Civilitie we see refin'd: the kiss
Which at the face began, transplanted is,
Since to the hand, since to the Imperial knee,
Now at the Papal foot delights to be:
If Kings think that the nearer way, and do
Rise from the foot, Lovers may do so too;
For as free Spheres move faster far than can
Birds, whom the air resists, so may that man

Which goes this empty and Ætherial way,
Than if at beauties elements he stay.
Rich Nature hath in women wisely made
Two purses, and their mouths aversely laid:
They then, which to the lower tribute owe,
That way which that Exchequer looks, must go:
He which doth not, his error is as great,
As who by Clyster gave the Stomack meat.

ELEGIE XIX

TO HIS MISTRIS GOING TO BED

Come, Madam, come, all rest my powers defie,
Until I labour, I in labour lie.
The foe oft-times having the foe in sight,
Is tir'd with standing though he never fight.
Off with that girdle, like heavens Zone glistering,
But a far fairer world incompassing.
Unpin that spangled breastplate which you wear,
That th'eyes of busie fooles may be stopt there.
Unlace your self, for that harmonious chyme,
Tells me from you, that now it is bed time.
Off with that happy busk, which I envie,
That still can be, and still can stand so nigh.
Your gown going off, such beautious state reveals,
As when from flowry meads th'hills shadow steales.
Off with that wyerie Coronet and shew
The haiery Diademe which on you doth grow:
Now off with those shooes, and then safely tread
In this loves hallow'd temple, this soft bed.
In such white robes, heaven's Angels us'd to be
Receavd by men; Thou Angel bringst with thee

A heaven like Mahomets Paradice; and though
Ill spirits walk in white, we easly know,
By this these Angels from an evil sprite,
Those set our hairs, but these our flesh upright.

    Licence my roaving hands, and let them go,
Before, behind, between, above, below.
O my America! my new-found-land,
My kingdome, safeliest when with one man man'd,
My Myne of precious stones, My Emperie,
How blest am I in this discovering thee!
To enter in these bonds, is to be free;
Then where my hand is set, my seal shall be.

    Full nakedness! All joyes are due to thee,
As souls unbodied, bodies uncloth'd must be,
To taste whole joyes. Gems which you women use
Are like Atlanta's balls, cast in mens views,
That when a fools eye lighteth on a Gem,
His earthly soul may covet theirs, not them.
Like pictures, or like books gay coverings made
For lay-men, are all women thus array'd;
Themselves are mystick books, which only wee
(Whom their imputed grace will dignifie)
Must see reveal'd. Then since that I may know;
As liberally, as to a Midwife, shew
Thy self: cast all, yea, this white lynnen hence,
Here is no pennance, much less innocence.

    To teach thee, I am naked first; why then
What needst thou have more covering than a man.

EPITHALAMIONS

AN EPITHALAMION, OR MARIAGE SONG
on the Lady Elizabeth, *and* Count Palatine
being married on St Valentines day[1]

I

Haile Bishop Valentine, whose day this is,
  All the Aire is thy Diocis,
  And all the chirping Choristers
And other birds are thy Parishioners,
   Thou marryest every yeare
The Lirique Larke, and the grave whispering Dove,
The Sparrow that neglects his life for love,
The household Bird, with the red stomacher,
   Thou mak'st the black bird speed as soone,
As doth the Goldfinch, or the Halcyon;
The husband cocke lookes out, and straight is sped,
And meets his wife, which brings her feather-bed.
This day more cheerfully than ever shine,
This day, which might enflame thy self, Old Valentine.

II

Till now, Thou warmd'st with multiplying loves
  Two larkes, two sparrowes, or two Doves,
  All that is nothing unto this,
For thou this day couplest two Phœnixes;

---

1. Elizabeth (1596–1662), eldest daughter of James I and Anne of Denmark, married, 1613, the Elector Palatine Frederick V, an occasion celebrated by all the principal poets of the day. As Queen of Bohemia, from which she was exiled in 1620, she acquired an almost legendary fame as a romantic figure whom no adversity could daunt.

Thou mak'st a Taper see
What the sunne never saw, and what the Arke
(Which was of foules, and beasts, the cage, and park,)
Did not containe, one bed containes, through Thee,
        Two Phœnixes, whose joyned breasts
Are unto one another mutuall nests,
Where motion kindles such fires, as shall give
Yong Phœnixes, and yet the old shall live.
Whose love and courage never shall decline,
But make the whole year through, thy day, O Valentine.

III

Up then faire Phœnix Bride, frustrate the Sunne,
        Thy selfe from thine affection
        Takest warmth enough, and from thine eye
All lesser birds will take their Jollitie.
        Up, up, faire Bride, and call,
Thy starres, from out their severall boxes, take
Thy Rubies, Pearles, and Diamonds forth, and make
Thy selfe a constellation, of them All,
        And by their blazing, signifie,
That a Great Princess falls, but doth not die;
Bee thou a new starre, that to us portends
Ends of much wonder; And be Thou those ends.
Since thou dost this day in new glory shine,
May all men date Records, from this thy Valentine.

IIII

Come forth, come forth, and as one glorious flame
        Meeting Another, growes the same,
        So meet thy Fredericke, and so
To an unseparable union growe.
        Since separation
Falls not on such things as are infinite,

Nor things which are but one, can disunite,
You'are twice inseparable, great, and one;
     Goe then to where the Bishop staies,
To make you one, his way, which divers waies
Must be effected; and when all is past,
And that you'are one, by hearts and hands made fast,
You two have one way left, your selves to'entwine,
Besides this Bishops knot, or Bishop Valentine.

V

But oh, what ailes the Sunne, that here he staies,
     Longer to day, than other daies?
     Staies he new light from these to get?
And finding here such store, is loth to set?
     And why doe you two walke,
So slowly pac'd in this procession?
Is all your care but to be look'd upon,
And be to others spectacle, and talke?
     The feast, with gluttonous delaies,
Is eaten, and too long their meat they praise,
The masquers come too late, and'I thinke, will stay,
Like Fairies, till the Cock crow them away.
Alas, did not Antiquity assigne
A night, as well as day, to thee, O Valentine?

VI

They did, and night is come; and yet wee see
     Formalities retarding thee.
     What meane these Ladies, which (as though
They were to take a clock in peeces,) goe
     So nicely about the Bride;
A Bride, before a good night could be said,
Should vanish from her cloathes, into her bed,
As Soules from bodies steale, and are not spy'd.

But now she is laid; What though shee bee?
Yet there are more delayes, For, where is he?
He comes, and passes through Spheare after Spheare,
First her sheetes, then her Armes, then any where.
Let not this day, then, but this night be thine,
Thy day was but the eve to this, O Valentine.

VII

Here lyes a shee Sunne, and a hee Moone here,
  She gives the best light to his Spheare,
  Or each is both, and all, and so
They unto one another nothing owe,
  And yet they doe, but are
So just and rich in that coyne which they pay,
That neither would, nor needs forbeare nor stay;
Neither desires to be spar'd, nor to spare,
  They quickly pay their debt, and then
Take no acquittances, but pay again;
They pay, they give, they lend, and so let fall
No such occasion to be liberall.
More truth, more courage in these two do shine,
Than all thy turtles have, and sparrows, Valentine.

VIII

And by this act of these two Phenixes
  Nature againe restored is,
  For since these two are two no more,
Ther's but one Phenix still, as was before.
  Rest now at last, and wee
As Satyres watch the Sunnes uprise, will stay
Waiting, when your eyes opened, let out day,
Onely desir'd, because your face wee see;
  Others neare you shall whispering speake,
And wagers lay, at which side day will breake,

And win by'observing, then, whose hand it is
That opens first a curtaine, hers or his;
This will be tryed to morrow after nine,
Till which houre, wee thy day enlarge, O Valentine.

EPITHALAMION MADE AT
LINCOLNES INNE[1]

The Sun-beames in the East are spred,
Leave, leave, faire Bride, your solitary bed,
　No more shall you returne to it alone,
It nourseth sadnesse, and your bodies print,
Like to a grave, the yielding downe doth dint;
　　　You and your other you meet there anon;
　　　　Put forth, put forth that warme balme-breathing thigh,
Which when next time you in these sheets will smother,
　　There it must meet another,
　　　　　Which never was, but must be, oft, more nigh;
Come glad from thence, goe gladder than you came,
To day put on perfection, and a womans name.

Daughters of London, you which bee
Our Golden Mines, and furnish'd Treasurie,
　You which are Angels, yet still bring with you
Thousands of Angels on your mariage daies,
Help with your presence and devise to praise
　These rites, which also unto you grow due;
　　Conceitedly dresse her, and be assign'd,
By you, fit place for every flower and jewell,
　　Make her for love fit fewell
　　　　　As gay as Flora, and as rich as Inde;
So may shee faire, rich, glad, and in nothing lame,
To day put on perfection, and a womans name.

1. Written after 1592, when Donne entered Lincoln's Inn as a student. It
is not known whose marriage he was celebrating.

And you frolique Patricians,
Sonnes of these Senators, wealths deep oceans,
  Ye painted courtiers, barrels of others wits,
Yee country men, who but your beasts love none,
Yee of those fellowships whereof hee's one,
  Of study and play made strange Hermaphrodits,
  Here shine; This Bridegroom to the Temple bring.
Loe, in yon path which store of straw'd flowers graceth,
  The sober virgin paceth;
      Except my sight faile, 'tis no other thing;
Weep not nor blush, here is no griefe nor shame,
To day put on perfection, and a womans name.

Thy two-leav'd gates faire Temple unfold,
And these two in thy sacred bosome hold,
  Till, mystically joyn'd, but one they bee;
Then may thy leane and hunger-starved wombe
Long time expect their bodies and their tombe,
  Long after their owne parents fatten thee.
  All elder claimes, and all cold barrennesse,
All yeelding to new loves bee far for ever,
    Which might these two dissever,
      All wayes all th'other may each one possesse;
For, the best Bride, best worthy of praise and fame,
To day puts on perfection, and a womans name.

Oh winter dayes bring much delight,
Not for themselves, but for they soon bring night;
  Other sweets wait thee than these diverse meats,
Other disports than dancing jollities,
Other love tricks than glancing with the eyes,
  But that the Sun still in our halfe Spheare sweates;
  Hee flies in winter, but he now stands still.
Yet shadowes turne; Noone point he hath attain'd,

His steeds nill bee restrain'd,
    But gallop lively downe the Westerne hill;
Thou shalt, when he hath runne the worlds half frame,
To night put on perfection, and a womans name.

The amorous evening starre is rose,
Why then should not our amorous starre inclose
    Her selfe in her wish'd bed? Release your strings
Musicians, and dancers take some truce
With these your pleasing labours, for great use
    As much wearinesse as perfection brings;
      You, and not only you, but all toyl'd beasts
Rest duly; at night all their toyles are dispensed;
But in their beds commenced
    Are other labours, and more dainty feasts;
She goes a maid, who, lest she turne the same,
To night puts on perfection, and a womans name.

Thy virgins girdle now untie,
And in thy nuptiall bed (loves altar) lye
    A pleasing sacrifice; now dispossesse
Thee of these chaines and robes which were put on
T'adorne the day, not thee; for thou, alone,
    Like vertue'and truth, art best in nakednesse;
      This bed is onely to virginitie
A grave, but, to a better state, a cradle;
Till now thou wast but able
    To be what now thou art; then that by thee
No more be said, *I may bee*, but, *I am*,
To night put on perfection, and a womans name.

Even like a faithfull man content,
That this life for a better should be spent,
    So, shee a mothers rich stile doth preferre,

And at the Bridegroomes wish'd approach doth lye,
Like an appointed lambe, when tenderly
   The priest comes on his knees t'embowell her;
     Now sleep or watch with more joy; and O light
Of heaven, to morrow rise thou hot, and early;
This Sun will love so dearely
     Her rest, that long, long we shall want her sight;
Wonders are wrought, for shee which had no maime,
To night puts on perfection, and a womans name.

SATYRES

SATYRE I

[On London Society]

Away thou fondling motley humorist,
Leave mee, and in this standing woodden chest,
Consorted with these few bookes, let me lye
In prison, and here be coffin'd, when I dye;
Here are Gods conduits, grave Divines; and here
Natures Secretary, the Philosopher;
And jolly Statesmen, which teach how to tie
The sinewes of a cities mistique bodie;
Here gathering Chroniclers, and by them stand
Giddie fantastique Poëts of each land.
Shall I leave all this constant company,
And follow headlong, wild uncertaine thee?
First sweare by thy best love in earnest
(If thou which lov'st all, canst love any best)
Thou wilt not leave mee in the middle street,
Though some more spruce companion thou dost meet,
Not though a Captaine do come in thy way
Bright parcell gilt, with forty dead mens pay,
Not though a briske perfum'd piert Courtier
Deigne with a nod, thy courtesie to answer.
Nor come a velvet Justice with a long
Great traine of blew coats, twelve, or fourteen strong,
Wilt thou grin or fawne on him, or prepare
A speech to Court his beautious sonne and heire!
For better or worse take mee, or leave mee:
To take, and leave mee is adultery.

Oh monstrous, superstitious puritan,
Of refin'd manners, yet ceremoniall man,
That when thou meet'st one, with enquiring eyes
Dost search, and like a needy broker prize
The silke, and gold he weares, and to that rate
So high or low, dost raise thy formall hat:
That wilt comfort none, untill thou have knowne
What lands hee hath in hope, or of his owne,
As though all thy companions should make thee
Jointures, and marry thy deare company.
Why should'st thou (that dost not onely approve,
But in ranke itchie lust, desire, and love
The nakednesse and barenesse to enjoy,
Of thy plumpe muddy whore, or prostitute boy)
Hate vertue, though shee be naked, and bare?
At birth, and death, our bodies naked are;
And till our Soules be unapparrelled
Of bodies, they from blisse are banished.
Mans first blest state was naked, when by sinne
Hee lost that, yet hee was cloath'd but in beasts skin,
And in this coarse attire, which I now weare,
With God, and with the Muses I conferre.
But since thou like a contrite penitent,
Charitably warn'd of thy sinnes, dost repent
These vanities, and giddinesses, loe
I shut my chamber doore, and come, lets goe.
But sooner may a cheape whore, who hath beene
Worne by as many severall men in sinne,
As are black feathers, or musk-colour hose,
Name her childs right true father, 'mongst all those:
Sooner may one guesse, who shall beare away
The Infanta of London,[1] Heire to an India;
And sooner may a gulling weather Spie

1. No particular heiress is intended.

By drawing forth heavens Scheme tell certainly
What fashioned hats, or ruffes, or suits next yeare
Our subtile-witted antique youths will weare;
Than thou, when thou depart'st from mee, canst show
Whither, why, when, or with whom thou wouldst go.
But how shall I be pardon'd my offence
That thus have sinn'd against my conscience?
Now we are in the street; He first of all
Improvidently proud, creepes to the wall,
And so imprisoned, and hem'd in by mee
Sells for a little state his libertie;
Yet though he cannot skip forth now to greet
Every fine silken painted foole we meet,
He them to him with amorous smiles allures,
And grins, smacks, shrugs, and such an itch endures,
As prentises, or schoole-boyes which doe know
Of some gay sport abroad, yet dare not goe.
And as fidlers stop lowest, at highest sound,
So to the most brave, stoops hee nigh'st the ground.
But to a grave man, he doth move no more
Than the wise politique horse[1] would heretofore,
Or thou O Elephant or Ape[2] wilt doe,
When any names the King of Spaine to you.
Now leaps he upright, Joggs me, and cryes, 'Do you see
Yonder well favoured youth?' 'Which?' 'Oh, 'tis hee
That dances so divinely'; 'Oh,' said I,
'Stand still, must you dance here for company?'
Hee droopt, wee went, till one (which did excell
Th'Indians, in drinking his Tobacco well)
Met us; they talk'd; I whispered, 'let'us goe,
'T may be you smell him not, truely I doe;'
He heares not mee, but, on the other side

1. Morocco, a celebrated performing horse.
2. An allusion to exotic animals on show in London c. 1594.

A many-coloured Peacock having spide,
Leaves him and mee; I for my lost sheep stay;
He followes, overtakes, goes on the way,
Saying, 'him whom I last left, all repute
For his device, in hansoming a sute,
To judge of lace, pinke, panes, print, cut, and pleate
Of all the Court, to have the best conceit;'
'Our dull Comedians want him, let him goe;
But Oh, God strengthen thee, why stoop'st thou so?'
'Why? he hath travayld;' 'Long?' 'No; but to me
(Which understand none,)[1] he doth seeme to be
Perfect French, and Italian;' I replyed,
'So is the Poxe;' He answered not, but spy'd
More men of sort, of parts, and qualities;
At last his Love he in a windowe spies,
And like light dew exhal'd, he flings from mee
Violently ravish'd to his lechery.
Many were there, he could command no more;
Hee quarrell'd, fought, bled; and turn'd out of dore
  Directly came to mee hanging the head,
  And constantly a while must keepe his bed.

SATYRE II

[On Lawyers]

Sir; though (I thanke God for it) I do hate
Perfectly all this towne, yet there's one state
In all ill things so excellently best,
That hate, toward them, breeds pitty towards the rest.
Though Poëtry indeed be such a sinne
As I thinke that brings dearth, and Spaniards in,
Though like the Pestilence and old fashion'd love,

1. An 'aside', presumably, by the poet interrupting his companion's answer
to the enquiry 'Long?'

Ridlingly it catch men; and doth remove
Never, till it be sterv'd out; yet their state
Is poore, disarm'd, like Papists, not worth hate.
One, (like a wretch, which at Barre judg'd as dead,
Yet prompts him which stands next, and cannot reade,
And saves his life) gives ideot actors meanes
(Starving himselfe) to live by his labor'd sceanes;
As in some Organ, Puppits dance above
And bellows pant below, which them do move.[1]
One would move Love by rithmes; but witchcrafts charms
Bring not now their old feares, nor their old harmes:
Rammes, and slings now are seely battery,
Pistolets are the best Artillerie.
And they who write to Lords, rewards to get,
Are they not like singers at doores for meat?
And they who write, because all write, have still
That excuse for writing, and for writing ill;
But hee is worst, who (beggarly) doth chaw
Others wits fruits, and in his ravenous maw
Rankly digested, doth those things out-spue,
As his owne things; and they are his owne, 'tis true,
For if one eate my meate, though it be knowne
The meate was mine, th'excrement is his owne:
But these do mee no harme, nor they which use
To out-swive Dildoes, and out-usure Jewes;
To out-drinke the sea, to out-sweare the Letanie;
Who with sinnes all kindes as familiar bee
As Confessors; and for whose sinfull sake,
Schoolemen new tenements in hell must make:
Whose strange sinnes, Canonists could hardly tell
In which Commandements large receit they dwell.
But these punish themselves; the insolence
Of Coscus onely breeds my just offence,

1. An oblique allusion to contemporary dramatic poets.

Whom time (which rots all, and makes botches poxe,
And plodding on, must make a calfe an oxe)
Hath made a Lawyer, which was (alas) of late
But a scarce Poët; jollier of this state,
Than are new benefic'd ministers, he throwes
Like nets, or lime-twigs, wheresoever he goes,
His title of Barrister, on every wench,
And wooes in language of the Pleas, and Bench:
'A motion, Lady'; 'Speake Coscus'; 'I have beene
In love, ever since *tricesimo* of the Queene,
Continuall claimes I have made, injunctions got
To stay my rivals suit, that hee should not
Proceed'; 'spare mee'; 'In Hillary terme I went,
You said, If I return'd next size in Lent,
I should be in remitter of your grace;
In th'interim my letters should take place
Of affidavits:' words, words, which would teare
The tender labyrinth of a soft maids eare,
More, more, than ten Sclavonians scolding, more
Than when winds in our ruin'd Abbeyes rore.
When sicke with Poëtrie, and possest with muse
Thou wast, and mad, I hop'd; but men which chuse
Law practise for meere gaine, bold soule, repute
Worse than imbrothel'd strumpets prostitute.
Now like an owlelike watchman, hee must walke
His hand still at a bill, now he must talke
Idly, like prisoners, which whole months will sweare
That onely suretiship hath brought them there
And to every suitor lye in every thing,
Like a Kings favourite, yea like a King;
Like a wedge in a blocke, wring to the barre,
Bearing-like[1] Asses; and more shamelesse farre

1. The reading '[Braying] like' has been suggested as an elucidation of this obscure passage.

Than carted whores, lye, to the grave Judge; for
Bastardy abounds not in Kings titles, nor
Symonie and Sodomy in Churchmens lives,
As these things do in him; by these he thrives.
Shortly (as the sea) hee will compasse all our land,
From Scots, to Wight; from Mount, to Dover strand.
And spying heires melting with luxurie,
Satan will not joy at their sinnes, as hee.
For as a thrifty wench scrapes kitching-stuffe,
And barrelling the droppings, and the snuffe,
Of wasting candles, which in thirty yeare
(Relique-like kept) perchance buyes wedding geare;
Peecemeale he gets lands, and spends as much time
Wringing each Acre, as men pulling prime.
In parchments then, large as his fields, hee drawes
Assurances, bigge, as gloss'd civill lawes,
So huge, that men (in our times forwardnesse)
Are Fathers of the Church for writing lesse.
These hee writes not; nor for these written payes,
Therefore spares no length; as in those first dayes
When Luther was profest, He did desire
Short *Pater nosters*, saying as a Fryer
Each day his beads, but having left those lawes,
Addes to Christs prayer, the Power and glory clause.
But when he sells or changes land, he'impaires
His writings, and (unwatch'd) leaves out, *ses heires*,
As slily as any Commenter goes by
Hard words, or sense; or in Divinity
As controverters, in vouch'd Texts, leave out
Shrewd words, which might against them cleare the doubt.
Where are those spred woods which cloth'd heretofore
Those bought lands? not built, nor burnt within dore.
Where's th'old landlords troops, and almes? In great hals
Carthusian fasts, and fulsome Bachanalls

Equally I hate; meanes blesse; in rich mens homes
I bid kill some beasts, but no Hecatombs,
None starve, none surfet so; But (Oh) we allow,
Good workes as good, but out of fashion now,
Like old rich wardrops; but my words none drawes
Within the vast reach of th'huge statute lawes.

SATYRE III

[On Religion]

Kinde pitty chokes my spleene; brave scorn forbids
Those teares to issue which swell my eye-lids;
I must not laugh, nor weepe sinnes, and be wise,
Can railing then cure these worne maladies?
Is not our Mistresse faire Religion,
As worthy of all our Soules devotion,
As vertue was to the first blinded age?
Are not heavens joyes as valiant to asswage
Lusts, as earths honour was to them? Alas,
As wee do them in meanes, shall they surpasse
Us in the end, and shall thy fathers spirit
Meete blinde Philosophers in heaven, whose merit
Of strict life may be imputed faith, and heare
Thee, whom hee taught so easie wayes and neare
To follow, damn'd? O if thou dar'st, feare this;
This feare great courage, and high valour is.
Dar'st thou ayd mutinous Dutch, and dar'st thou lay
Thee in ships woodden Sepulchers, a prey
To leaders rage, to stormes, to shot, to dearth?
Dar'st thou dive seas, and dungeons of the earth?
Hast thou couragious fire to thaw the ice
Of frozen North discoveries? and thrise
Colder than Salamanders, like divine
Children in th'oven, fires of Spaine, and the line,

Whose countries limbecks to our bodies bee,
Canst thou for gaine beare? and must every hee
Which cryes not, Goddesse, to thy Mistresse, draw,
Or eate thy poysonous words? courage of straw!
O desperate coward, wilt thou seeme bold, and
To thy foes and his (who made thee to stand
Sentinell in his worlds garrison) thus yeeld,
And for the forbidden warres, leave th'appointed field?
Know thy foes: The foule Devill (whom thou
Strivest to please,) for hate, not love, would allow
Thee faine, his whole Realme to be quit; and as
The worlds all parts wither away and passe,
So the worlds selfe, thy other lov'd foe, is
In her decrepit wayne, and thou loving this,
Dost love a withered and worne strumpet; last,
Flesh (it selfes death) and joyes which flesh can taste,
Thou lovest; and thy faire goodly soule, which doth
Give this flesh power to taste joy, thou dost loath.
Seeke true religion. O where? Mirreus
Thinking her unhous'd here, and fled from us,
Seekes her at Rome; there, because hee doth know
That shee was there a thousand yeares agoe,
He loves her ragges so, as wee here obey
The statecloth where the Prince sate yesterday.
Crantz to such brave Loves will not be inthrall'd,
But loves her onely, who at Geneva is call'd
Religion, plaine, simple, sullen, yong,
Contemptuous, yet unhansome; As among
Lecherous humors, there is one that judges
No wenches wholsome, but coarse country drudges.
Graius stayes still at home here, and because
Some Preachers, vile ambitious bauds, and lawes
Still new like fashions, bid him thinke that shee
Which dwels with us, is onely perfect, hee

Imbraceth her, whom his Godfathers will
Tender to him, being tender, as Wards still
Take such wives as their Guardians offer, or
Pay valewes. Carelesse Phrygius doth abhorre
All, because all cannot be good, as one
Knowing some women whores, dares marry none.
Graccus loves all as one, and thinks that so
As women do in divers countries goe
In divers habits, yet are still one kinde,
So doth, so is Religion; and this blind-
nesse too much light breeds; but unmoved thou
Of force must one, and forc'd but one allow;
And the right; aske thy father which is shee,
Let him aske his; though truth and falsehood bee
Neare twins, yet truth a little elder is;
Be busie to seeke her, beleeve mee this,
Hee's not of none, nor worst, that seekes the best.
To adore, or scorne an image, or protest,
May all be bad; doubt wisely; in strange way
To stand inquiring right, is not to stray;
To sleepe, or runne wrong, is. On a huge hill,
Cragged, and steep, Truth stands, and hee that will
Reach her, about must, and about must goe;
And what the hills suddennes resists, winne so;
Yet strive so, that before age, deaths twilight,
Thy Soule rest, for none can worke in that night.
To will, implyes delay, therefore now doé:
Hard deeds, the bodies paines; hard knowledge too
The mindes indeavours reach, and mysteries
Are like the Sunne, dazling, yet plaine to all eyes.
Keepe the truth which thou hast found; men do not stand
In so ill case here, that God hath with his hand
Sign'd Kings blanck-charters to kill whom they hate,
Nor are they Vicars, but hangmen to Fate.

Foole and wretch, wilt thou let thy Soule be tyed
To mans lawes, by which she shall not be tryed
At the last day? Oh, will it then boot thee
To say a Philip, or a Gregory,
A Harry, or a Martin taught thee this?
Is not this excuse for mere contraries,
Equally strong? cannot both sides say so?
That thou mayest rightly obey power, her bounds know;
Those past, her nature, and name is chang'd; to be
Then humble to her is idolatrie.
As streames are, Power is; those blest flowers that dwell
At the rough streames calme head, thrive and do well,
But having left their roots, and themselves given
To the streames tyrannous rage, alas are driven
Through mills, and rockes, and woods, and at last, almost
Consum'd in going, in the sea are lost:
So perish Soules, which more chuse mens unjust
Power from God claym'd, than God himselfe to trust.

SATYRE IIII

[On the Court]

Well; I may now receive, and die; My sinne
Indeed is great, but I have beene in
A Purgatorie, such as fear'd hell is
A recreation to, and scarse map of this.
My minde, neither with prides itch, nor yet hath been
Poyson'd with love to see, or to bee seene,
I had no suit there, nor new suite to shew,
Yet went to Court; But as Glaze which did goe
To'a Masse in jest, catch'd, was faine to disburse
The hundred markes, which is the Statutes curse,
Before he scapt; So'it pleas'd my destinie
(Guilty of my sin of going), to thinke me

As prone to all ill, and of good as forget-
full, as proud, as lustfull, and as much in debt,
As vaine, as witlesse, and as false as they
Which dwell at Court, for once going that way.
Therefore I suffered this; Towards me did runne
A thing more strange, than on Niles slime, the Sunne
E'r bred; or all which into Noahs Arke came;
A thing, which would have pos'd Adam to name;
Stranger than seaven Antiquaries studies,
Than Africks Monsters, Guianaes rarities.
Stranger than strangers; One, who for a Dane,
In the Danes Massacre had sure beene slaine,
If he had liv'd then; And without helpe dies,
When next the Prentises 'gainst Strangers rise.
One, whom the watch at noone lets scarce goe by,
One, to whom, the examining Justice sure would cry,
'Sir, by your priesthood tell me what you are'.
His cloths were strange, though coarse; and black, though
  bare;
Sleeveless his jerkin was, and it had beene
Velvet, but 'twas now (so much ground was seene)
Become Tufftaffatie; and our children shall
See it plaine Rashe awhile, then nought at all.
This thing hath travail'd, and saith, speakes all tongues
And only knoweth what to all States belongs.
Made of th'Accents, and best phrase of all these,
He speakes one language; If strange meats displease,
Art can deceive, or hunger force my tast,
But Pedants motley tongue, souldiers bumbast,
Mountebankes drugtongue, nor the termes of law
Are strong enough preparatives, to draw
Me to beare this: yet I must be content
With his tongue, in his tongue, call'd complement:
In which he can win widdowes, and pay scores,

Make men speake treason, cosen subtlest whores,
Out-flatter favorites, or outlie either
Jovius, or Surius, or both together.
He names mee, and comes to mee; I whisper, 'God!
How have I sinn'd, that thy wraths furious rod,
This fellow chuseth me?' He saith, 'Sir,
I love your judgement; Whom doe you prefer,
For the best linguist?' And I seelily
Said, that I thought Calepines Dictionarie[1];
'Nay, but of men, most sweet Sir'; Beza then,
Some other Jesuites, and two reverend men
Of our two Academies, I named; There
He stopt mee, and said; 'Nay, your Apostles were
Good pretty linguists, and so Panurge was;
Yet a poore gentleman, all these may passe
By travaile'. Then, as if he would have sold
His tongue, he prais'd it, and such wonders told
That I was faine to say, 'If you'had liv'd, Sir,
Time enough to have been Interpreter
To Babells bricklayers, sure the Tower had stood.'
He adds, 'If of court life you knew the good,
You would leave lonenesse'. I said, 'not alone
My lonenesse is, but Spartanes fashion,
To teach by painting drunkarks, doth not last
Now; Aretines pictures have made few chast;
No more can Princes courts, though there be few
Better pictures of vice, teach me vertue;'
He, like to a high stretcht lute string squeakt, 'O Sir,
'Tis sweet to talke of Kings'. 'At Westminster,'
Said I, 'The man that keepes the Abbey tombes,
And for his price doth with who ever comes,
Of all our Harries, and our Edwards talke,
From King to King and all their kin can walke:

1. A famous polyglot dictionary.

Your eares shall heare nought, but Kings; your eyes meet
Kings only; The way to it, is Kingstreet."
He smack'd, and cry'd, 'He's base, Mechanique, coarse,
So are all your Englishmen in their discourse.
Are not your Frenchmen neate?' 'Mine? as you see,
I have but one Frenchman, looke, hee followes mee.'
'Certes they are neatly cloth'd; I, of this minde am,
Your only wearing is your Grogaram.'
'Not so Sir, I have more.' Under this pitch
He would not flie; I chaff'd him; But as Itch
Scratch'd into smart, and as blunt iron ground
Into an edge, hurts worse: So, I (foole) found,
Crossing hurt mee; To fit my sullennesse,
He to another key, his stile doth addresse,
And asks, 'what newes?' I tell him of new playes.
He takes my hand, and as a Still, which staies
A Sembriefe, 'twixt each drop, he nigardly,
As loth to enrich mee, so tells many a lie.
More than ten Hollensheads, or Halls, or Stowes,
Of triviall houshold trash he knowes; He knowes
When the Queene frown'd, or smil'd, and he knowes what
A subtle States-man may gather of that;
He knowes who loves; whom; and who by poyson
Hasts to an Offices reversion;
He knowes who'hath sold his land, and now doth beg
A licence, old iron, bootes, shooes, and egge-
shels to transport; Shortly boyes shall not play
At span-counter, or blow-point, but they pay
Toll to some Courtier; And wiser than all us,
He knowes what Ladie is not painted; Thus
He with home-meats tries me; I belch, spue, spit,
Looke pale, and sickly, like a Patient; Yet
He thrusts on more; And as if he'd undertooke

1. Between Charing Cross and Westminster.

To say Gallo-Belgicus without booke
Speakes of all States, and deeds, that have been since
The Spaniards came, to the losse of Amyens.
Like a bigge wife, at sight of loathed meat,
Readie to travaile: So I sigh, and sweat
To heare this Makeron[1] talke: In vaine; for yet,
Either my humour, or his owne to fit,
He like a privilegd'd spie, whom nothing can
Discredit, Libells now 'gainst each great man.
He names a price for every office paid;
He saith, our warres thrive ill, because delai'd;
That offices are entail'd, and that there are
Perpetuities of them, lasting as farre
As the last day; And that great officers,
Doe with the Pirates share, and Dunkirkers.
Who wasts in meat, in clothes, in horse, he notes;
Who loves whores, who boyes, and who goats.
I more amas'd than Circes prisoners, when
They felt themselves turne beasts, felt my selfe then
Becomming Traytor, and mee thought I saw
One of our Giant Statutes ope his jaw
To sucke me in; for hearing him, I found
That as burnt venome Leachers do grow sound
By giving others their soares, I might growe
Guilty, and he free: Therefore I did shew
All signes of loathing; But since I am in,
I must pay mine, and my forefathers sinne
To the last farthing; Therefore to my power
Toughly and stubbornly I beare this crosse; But the'houre
Of mercy now was come; He tries to bring
Me to pay a fine to scape his torturing,
And saies, 'Sir, can you spare me'; I said, 'willingly';

1. From the Italian *maccherone* – a buffoon; a blockhead, dolt. The *Oxford Dictionary* quotes this passage for its earliest use in English.

'Nay, Sir, can you spare me a crowne?' Thankfully I
Gave it, as Ransome; But as fidlers, still,
Though they be paid to be gone, yet needs will
Thrust one more jigge upon you: so did hee
With his long complementall thankes vexe me.
But he is gone, thankes to his needy want,
And the prerogative of my Crowne: Scant
His thankes were ended, when I, (which did see
All the court fill'd with more strange things than hee)
Ran from thence with such or more haste, than one
Who feares more actions, doth make from prison.
At home in wholesome solitarinesse
My precious soule began, the wretchednesse
Of suiters at court to mourne, and a trance
Like his, who[1] dreamt he saw hell, did advance
It selfe on mee, Such men as he saw there,
I saw at court, and worse, and more; Low feare
Becomes the guiltie, not the accuser; Then,
Shall I, nones slave, of high borne, or rais'd men
Feare frownes? And, my Mistresse Truth, betray thee
To th'huffing braggart, puft Nobility?
No, no, Thou which since yesterday hast beene
Almost about the whole world, hast thou seene,
O Sunne, in all thy journey, Vanitie,
Such as swells the bladder of our court? I
Thinke he which made your waxen garden,[2] and
Transported it from Italy to stand
With us, at London, flouts our Presence, for
Just such gay painted things, which no sappe, nor
Tast have in them, ours are; And naturall
Some of the stocks are, their fruits, bastard all.

1. *i.e.* Dante.
2. Miniature gardens exhibited in London at the time by travelling Italian
showmen.

'Tis ten a clock and past; All whom the Mews,
Baloune,[1] Tennis, Dyet, or the stewes,
Had all the morning held, now the second
Time made ready, that day, in flocks, are found
In the Presence, and I, (God pardon mee.)
As fresh, and sweet their Apparrells be, as bee
The fields they sold to buy them: For a King
Those hose are, cry the flatterers; And bring
Them next weeke to the Theatre to sell;
Wants reach all states; Me seemes they doe as well
At stage, as court; All are players; who e'r lookes
(For themselves dare not goe) o'r Cheapside books,
Shall finde their wardrops Inventory. Now,
The Ladies come; As Pirats, which doe know
That there came weak ships fraught with Cutchannel,[2]
The men board them; and praise, as they thinke, well,
Their beauties; they the mens wits; Both are bought.
Why good wits ne'r weare scarlet gownes, I thought
This cause, These men, mens wits for speeches buy,
And women buy all reds which scarlets die.
He call'd her beauty limetwigs, her haire net;
She feares her drugs ill laid, her haire loose set.
Would not Heraclitus laugh to see Macrine,
From hat to shooe, himselfe at doore refine,
As if the Presence were a Moschite,[3] and lift
His skirts and hose, and call his clothes to shrift,
Making them confesse not only mortall
Great staines and holes in them; but veniall
Feathers and dust, wherewith they fornicate:
And then by *Durers* rules survay the state
Of his each limbe, and with strings the odds trye

1. A form of Medicine Ball.
2. *i.e.* Cochineal.
3. Obsolete form of 'Mosque'. (The *Oxford Dictionary*, quoting this passage.)

Of his neck to his legge, and wast to thighe.
So in immaculate clothes, and Symetrie
Perfect as circles, with such nicetie
As a young Preacher at his first time goes
To preach, he enters, and a Lady which owes
Him not so much as good will, he arrests,
And unto her protests protests protests
So much as at Rome would serve to have throwne
Ten Cardinalls into the Inquisition;
And whisperd by Jesu, so often, that A
Pursevant[1] would have ravish'd him away
For saying of our Ladies psalter; But 'tis fit
That they each other plague, they merit it.
But here comes Glorius that will plague them both,
Who, in the other extreme, only doth
Call a rough carelessenesse, good fashion;
Whose cloak his spurres teare; whom he spits on
He cares not, his ill words doe no harme
To him; he rusheth in, as if arme, arme,
He meant to crie; And though his face be as ill
As theirs which in old hangings whip Christ, still
He strives to looke worse, he keepes all in awe;
Jeasts like a licenc'd foole, commands like law.
Tyr'd, now I leave this place, and but pleas'd so
As men which from gaoles to'execution goe,
Goe through the great chamber (why is it hung
With the seaven deadly sinnes?). Being among
Those Askaparts,[2] men big enough to throw
Charing Crosse for a barre, men that doe know
No token of worth, but Queenes man, and fine
Living, barrells of beefe, flaggons of wine;

1. Some MS. copies read 'Topcliffe' *i.e.* Richard Topcliffe, a notoriously
cruel anti-Catholic agent and informer of the period.
2. Askapart, a legendary giant, 30 feet high.

I shooke like a spyed Spie. Preachers which are
Seas of Wit and Arts, you can, then dare,
Drowne the sinnes of this place, for, for mee
Which am but a scarce brooke, it enough shall bee
To wash the staines away; Although I yet
With *Macchabees* modestie,[1] the knowne merit
Of my worke lessen; yet some wise man shall,
I hope, esteeme my writs Canonicall.

1. *v.* 2 Maccabees, xv. 38.

VERSE LETTERS TO
SEVERALL PERSONAGES

TO MR CHRISTOPHER BROOKE[1]

THE STORME[2]

Thou which art I, ('tis nothing to be soe)
Thou which art still thy selfe, by these shalt know
Part of our passage; And, a hand, or eye
By *Hilliard*[3] drawne, is worth an history,
By a worse painter made; and (without pride)
When by thy judgment they are dignifi'd,
My lines are such: 'Tis the preheminence
Of friendship onely to'impute excellence.
England to whom we'owe, what we be, and have,
Sad that her sonnes did seeke a forraine grave
(For, Fates, or Fortunes drifts none can soothsay,
Honour and misery have one face and way.)
From out her pregnant intrailes sigh'd a winde
Which at th'ayres middle marble roome did finde
Such strong resistance, that it selfe it threw
Downeward againe; and so when it did view
How in the port, our fleet deare time did leese,

1. *d.* 1628, poet, lawyer, and intimate friend of Donne's. He and his brother,
Rev. Samuel Brooke, connived in Donne's runaway marriage, and were
put under arrest for their pains.
2. This and the following poem were written at the time of the famous
Islands' Voyage, under Ralegh, Howard and Essex, in the summer of
1597. Donne took part in this expedition to intercept the Spanish silver
fleet.
3. Nicholas Hilliard, 1537–1619, the first English miniaturist. The portrait
of Donne, engraved by Marshall, has been attributed to him.

Withering like prisoners, which lye but for fees,
Mildly it kist our sailes, and, fresh and sweet,
As to a stomack sterv'd, whose insides meete,
Meate comes, it came; and swole our sailes, when wee
So joyd, as *Sara*'her swelling joy'd to see.
But 'twas but so kinde, as our countrimen,
Which bring friends one dayes way, and leave them then.
Then like two mighty Kings, which dwelling farre
Asunder, meet against a third to warre,
The South and West winds joyn'd, and, as they blew,
Waves like a rowling trench before them threw.
Sooner than you read this line, did the gale,
Like shot, not fear'd till felt, our sailes assaile;
And what at first was call'd a gust, the same
Hath now a stormes, anon a tempests name.
Jonas, I pitty thee, and curse those men,
Who when the storm rag'd most, did wake thee then;
Sleepe is paines easiest salve, and doth fulfill
All offices of death, except to kill.
But when I wakt, I saw, that I saw not;
Ay, and the Sunne, which should teach mee'had forgot
East, West, Day, Night, and I could onely say,
If'the world had lasted, now it had been day.
Thousands our noyses were, yet wee'mongst all
Could none by his right name, but thunder call:
Lightning was all our light, and it rain'd more
Than if the Sunne had drunke the sea before.
Some coffin'd in their cabbins lye,'equally
Griev'd that they are not dead, and yet must dye;
And as sin-burd'ned soules from graves will creepe,
At the last day, some forth their cabbins peepe:
And tremblingly'aske what newes, and doe heare so,
Like jealous hubands, what they would not know.
Some sitting on the hatches, would seeme there,

With hideous gazing to feare away feare.
Then note they the ships sicknesses, the Mast
Shak'd with this ague, and the Hold and Wast
With a salt dropsie clog'd, and all our tacklings
Snapping, like too-high-stretched treble strings.
And from our totterd sailes, ragges drop downe so,
As from one hang'd in chaines, a yeare agoe.
Even our Ordinance plac'd for our defence,
Strive to breake loose, and scape away from thence.
Pumping hath tir'd our men, and what's the gaine?
Seas into seas throwne, we suck in againe;
Hearing hath deaf'd our saylers; and if they
Knew how to heare, there's none knowes what to say.
Compar'd to these stormes, death is but a qualme,
Hell somewhat lightsome, and the'Bermuda calme.
Darknesse, lights elder brother, his birth-right
Claims o'er this world, and to heaven hath chas'd light.
All things are one, and that one none can be,
Since all formes, uniforme deformity
Doth cover, so that wee, except God say
Another *Fiat*, shall have no more day.
So violent, yet long these furies bee,
That though thine absence sterve me,'I wish not thee.

THE CALME

Our storme is past, and that storms tyrannous rage,
A stupid calme, but nothing it, doth swage.
The fable is inverted, and farre more
A blocke afflicts, now, than a storke before.
Stormes chafe, and soon weare out themselves, or us;
In calmes, Heaven laughs to see us languish thus.
As steady'as I can wish, that my thoughts were,
Smooth as thy mistresse glasse, or what shines there,

The sea is now. And, as the Iles which wee
Seeke, when wee can move, our ships rooted bee.
As water did in stormes, now pitch runs out:
As lead, when a fir'd Church becomes one spout.
And all our beauty, and our trimme, decayes,
Like courts removing, or like ended playes.
The fighting place now seamens ragges supply;
And all the tackling is a frippery.
No use of lanthornes; and in one place lay
Feathers and dust, to day and yesterday.[1]
Earths hollownesses, which the worlds lungs are,
Have no more winde than the upper valt of aire.
We can nor lost friends, nor sought foes recover,
But meteorlike, save that wee move not, hover.
Onely the Calenture[2] together drawes
Deare friends, which meet dead in great fishes jawes:
And on the hatches as on Altars lyes
Each one, his owne Priest, and owne Sacrifice.
Who live, that miracle do multiply
Where walkers in hot Ovens, doe not dye.
If in despite of these, wee swimme, that hath
No more refreshing, than our brimstone Bath,
But from the sea, into the ship we turne,
Like parboyl'd wretches, on the coales to burne.
Like *Bajazet* encag'd, the shepheards scoffe,
Or like slacke sinew'd *Sampson*, his haire off,
Languish our ships. Now, as a Miriade
Of Ants, durst th'Emperours lov'd snake invade,
The crawling Gallies, Sea-gaols, finny chips,
Might brave our Pinnaces, now bed-ridde ships.

---

1. Ben Jonson told Drummond of Hawthornden that he knew this couplet by heart.
2. 'A disease incident to sailors within the tropics, characterized by a delirium in which the patient, it is said, fancies the sea to be green fields, and desires to leap into it.' *Oxford Dictionary.*

Whether a rotten state, and hope of gaine,
Or to disuse mee from the queasie paine
Of being belov'd, and loving, or the thirst
Of honour, or faire death, out pusht mee first,
I lose my end: for here as well as I
A desperate may live, and a coward die.
Stagge, dogge, and all which from, or towards flies,
Is paid with life, or pray, or doing dyes.
Fate grudges us all, and doth subtly lay
A scourge,'gainst which wee all forget to pray,
He that at sea prayes for more winde, as well
Under the poles may begge cold, heat in hell.
What are wee then? How little more alas
Is man now, than before he was? he was
Nothing; for us, wee are for nothing fit;
Chance, or our selves still disproportion it.
Wee have no power, no will, no sense; I lye,
I should not then thus feele this miserie.

TO THE COUNTESSE OF HUNTINGDON[1]

That unripe side of earth, that heavy clime
That gives us man up now, like *Adams* time
Before he ate; mans shape, that would yet bee
(Knew they not it, and fear'd beasts companie)
So naked at this day, as though man there
From Paradise so great a distance were,
As yet the newes could not arrived bee
Of *Adams* tasting the forbidden tree;
Depriv'd of that free state which they were in,

1. First included in the canon of Donne's poems in 1929 (Nonesuch *Donne*).
Some lines appear to be lacking at the beginning. Elizabeth, daughter of
the Earl of Derby, was one of the great ladies who befriended Donne
and were celebrated in his verse. She married the 5th Earl of Huntingdon
in 1603 and died in 1633.

And wanting the reward, yet beare the sinne.

But, as from extreme hights who downward looks,
Sees men at childrens shapes, Rivers at brookes,
And loseth younger formes; so, to your eye,
These (Madame) that without your distance lie,
Must either mist, or nothing seeme to be,
Who are at home but wits mere *Atomi*.
But, I who can behold them move, and stay,
Have found my selfe to you, just their midway;
And now must pitty them; for, as they doe
Seeme sick to me, just so must I to you.
Yet neither will I vexe your eyes to see
A sighing Ode, nor crosse-arm'd Elegie.
I come not to call pitty from your heart,
Like some white-liver'd dotard that would part
Else from his slipperie soule with a faint groane,
And faithfully, (without you smil'd) were gone.
I cannot feele the tempest of a frowne,
I may be rais'd by love, but not throwne down.
Though I can pittie those sigh twice a day,
I hate that thing whispers it selfe away.
Yet since all love is fever, who to trees
Doth talke, doth yet in loves cold ague freeze.
'Tis love, but, with such fatall weaknesse made,
That it destroyes it selfe with its owne shade.
Who first look'd sad, griev'd, pin'd, and shew'd his paine,
Was he that first taught women, to disdaine.

As all things were one nothing, dull and weake,
Untill this raw disordered heape did breake,
And severall desires led parts away,
Water declin'd with earth, the ayre did stay,
Fire rose, and each from other but unty'd,
Themselves unprison'd were and purify'd:
So was love, first in vast confusion hid,

An unripe willingnesse which nothing did,
A thirst, an Appetite which had no ease,
That found a want, but knew not what would please.
What pretty innocence in those dayes mov'd!
Man ignorantly walk'd by her he lov'd;
Both sigh'd and enterchang'd a speaking eye,
Both trembled and were sick, both knew not why.
That naturall fearefulnesse that struck man dumbe,
Might well (those times consider'd) man become.
As all discoverers whose first assay
Findes but the place, after, the nearest way:
So passion is to womans love, about,
Nay, farther off, than when we first set out.
It is not love that sueth, or doth contend;
Love either conquers, or but meets a friend.
Man's better part consists of purer fire,
And findes it selfe allow'd, ere it desire.
Love is wise here, keepes home, gives reason sway,
And journeys not till it finde summer-way.
A weather-beaten Lover but once knowne,
Is sport for every girle to practise on.
Who strives through womans scornes, women to know,
Is lost, and seekes his shadow to outgoe;
It must be sicknesse, after one disdaine,
Though he be call'd aloud, to looke againe.
Let others sigh, and grieve; one cunning sleight
Shall freeze my Love to Christall in a night.
I can love first, and (if I winne) love still;
And cannot be remov'd, unlesse she will.
It is her fault if I unsure remaine,
Shee onely can untie, and binde againe.
The honesties of love with ease I doe,
But am no porter for a tedious woo.
  But (madame) I now thinke on you; and here

Where we are at our hights, you but appeare,
We are but clouds you rise from, our noone-ray
But a foule shadow, not your breake of day.
You are at first hand all that's faire and right,
And others good reflects but backe your light.
You are a perfectnesse, so curious hit,
That youngest flatteries doe scandall[1] it.
For, what is more doth what you are restraine,
And though beyond, is downe the hill againe.
We'have no next way to you, we crosse to it:
You are the straight line, thing prais'd, attribute;
Each good in you's a light; so many a shade
You make, and in them are your motions made.
These are your pictures to the life. From farre
We see you move, and here your *Zani's* are:
So that no fountaine good there is, doth grow
In you, but our dimme actions faintly shew.

　　Then finde I, if mans noblest part be love,
Your purest luster must that shadow move.
The soule with body, is a heaven combin'd
With earth, and for mans ease, but nearer joyn'd.
Where thoughts the starres of soule we understand,
We guesse not their large natures, but command.
And love in you, that bountie is of light,
That gives to all, and yet hath infinite.
Whose heat doth force us thither to intend,
But soule we finde too earthly to ascend,
'Till slow accesse hath made it wholy pure,
Able immortall clearnesse to endure.
Who dare aspire this journey with a staine,
Hath waight will force him headlong backe againe.
No more can impure man retaine and move
In that pure region of a worthy love,

　　　　　　　1. *i.e.* defame.

Than earthly substance can unforc'd aspire,
And leave his nature to converse with fire:
Such may have eye, and hand; may sigh, may speak;
But like swoln bubles, when they are high'st they break.

Though far removed Northerne fleets scarce finde
The Sunnes comfort; others thinke him too kinde.
There is an equall distance from her eye,
Men perish too farre off, and burne too nigh.
But as ayre takes the Sunne-beames equall bright
From the first Rayes, to his last opposite:
So able men, blest with a vertuous Love,
Remote or neare, or howsoe'r they move;
Their vertue breakes all clouds that might annoy,
There is no Emptinesse, but all is Joy.
He much profanes whom violent heats do move
To stile his wandring rage of passion, *Love*.
Love that imparts in every thing delight,
Is fain'd, which only tempts mans appetite.
Why love among the vertues is not knowne
Is, that love is them all contract in one.

TO SIR HENRY WOTTON[1]

Sir, more than kisses, letters mingle Soules;
For, thus friends absent speake. This ease controules
The tediousnesse of my life: But for these
I could ideate nothing, which could please,
But I should wither in one day, and passe
To'a bottle'of Hay, that am a locke of Grasse.
Life is a voyage, and in our lifes wayes

---

1. On a question debated whether life is best in the City, or in the Country, or at Court. Sir Henry Wotton (1568–1639), poet and diplomatist, was at Oxford with Donne and remained his close friend for life. When Donne died, Wotton, then Provost of Eton, was one of the few recipients, under his will, of a bloodstone seal.

Countries, Courts, Towns are Rockes, or Remoraes;
They breake or stop all ships, yet our state's such,
That though than pitch they staine worse, wee must touch,
If in the furnace of the even line,
Or under th'adverse icy poles thou pine,
Thou know'st two temperate Regions girded in,
Dwell there: But Oh, what refuge canst thou winne
Parch'd in the Court, and in the country frozen?
Shall cities, built of both extremes, be chosen?
Can dung and garlike be'a perfume? or can
A Scorpion and Torpedo cure a man?
Cities are worst of all three; of all three
(O knottie riddle) each is worst equally.
Cities are Sepulchers; they who dwell there
Are carcases, as if such there were.
And Courts are Theaters, where some men play
Princes, some slaves, all to one end, and of one clay.
The Country is a desert, where no good,
Gain'd (as habits, not borne,) is understood.
There men become beasts, and prone to more evils;
In cities blockes, and in a lewd court, devills.
As in the first Chaos confusedly
Each elements qualities were in the'other three;
So pride, lust, covetize, being severall
To these three places, yet all are in all,
And mingled thus, their issue incestuous.
Falshood is denizon'd. Virtue is barbarous.
Let no man say there, Virtues flintie wall
Shall locke vice in mee, I'll do none, but know all.
Men are spunges, which to poure out, receive,
Who know false play, rather than lose, deceive.
For in best understandings, sinne beganne,
Angels sinn'd first, then Devills, and then man.
Onely perchance beasts sinne not; wretched wee

Are beasts in all, but white integritie.
I thinke if men, which in these places live
Durst looke for themselves, and themselves retrive,
They would like strangers greet themselves, seeing then
Utopian youth, growne old Italian.

Be thou thine owne home, and in thy selfe dwell;
Inne any where, continuance maketh hell.
And seeing the snaile, which every where doth rome,
Carrying his owne house still, still is at home,
Follow (for he is easie pac'd) this snaile,
Bee thine owne Palace, or the world's thy gaole.
And in the worlds sea, do not like corke sleepe
Upon the waters face; nor in the deepe
Sinke like a lead without a line: but as
Fishes glide, leaving no print where they passe,
Nor making sound; so closely thy course goe,
Let men dispute, whether thou breathe, or no.
Onely'in this one thing, be no Galenist: To make
Courts hot ambitions wholesome, do not take
A dramme of Countries dulnesse; do not adde
Correctives, but as chymiques, purge the bad.[1]
But, Sir, I advise not you, I rather doe
Say o'er those lessons, which I learn'd of you:
Whom, free from German schismes, and lightnesse
Of France, and faire Italies faithlesnesse,
Having from these suck'd all they had of worth,
And brought home that faith, which you carried forth,
I throughly love. But if my selfe, I'have wonne
To know my rules, I have, and you have

DONNE.

1. The Galenists believed that deficiencies in any of the four 'humours' in
the body needed correction by drugs. The 'chymiques', or Paracelsians,
prescribed purging.

TO SIR HENRY GOODYERE[1]

Who makes the Past, a patterne for next yeare,
   Turnes no new leafe, but still the same things reads,
Seene things, he sees againe, heard things doth heare,
   And makes his life, but like a paire of beads.

A Palace, when'tis that, which it should be,
   Leaves growing, and stands such, or else decayes:
But hee which dwels there, is not so; for hee
   Strives to urge upward, and his fortune raise;

So had your body'her morning, hath her noone,
   And shall not better; her next change is night:
But her faire larger guest, to'whom Sun and Moone
   Are sparkes, and short liv'd, claimes another right.

The noble Soule by age growes lustier,
   Her appetite, and her digestion mend,
Wee must not sterve, nor hope to pamper her
   With womens milke, and pappe unto the end.

Provide you manlyer dyet; you have seene
   All libraries, which are Schools, Camps, and Courts;
But aske your Garners if you have not beene
   In harvests, too indulgent to your sports.

Would you redeeme it? then your selfe transplant
   A while from hence. Perchance outlandish ground
Beares no more wit, than ours, but yet more scant
   Are those diversions there, which here abound.

---

1. Sir Henry Goodyer (1571–1627) of Polesworth, *co.* Warwick, where he
was a genial host to the leading poets of his time. For some years after
1600 Donne and he corresponded regularly, sometimes as often as once a
week. His improvidence, as this verse-letter shows, was a matter of
concern to Donne.

To be a stranger hath that benefit,
 Wee can beginnings, but not habits choke.
Goe; whither? Hence; you get, if you forget;
 New faults, till they prescribe in us, are smoake.

Our soule, whose country'is heaven, and God her father,
 Into this world, corruptions sinke, is sent,
Yet, so much in her travaile she doth gather,
 That she returnes home, wiser than she went;

It payes you well, if it teach you to spare,
 And make you,'asham'd, to make your hawks praise,
  yours,
Which when herselfe she lessens in the aire,
 You then first say, that high enough she toures.

However, keepe the lively tast you hold
 Of God, love him as now, but feare him more,
And in your afternoones thinke what you told
 And promis'd him, at morning prayer before.

Let falshood like a discord anger you,
 Else be not froward. But why doe I touch
Things, of which none is in your practise new,
 And Tables[1] or fruit-trenchers teach as much;

But thus I make you keepe your promise Sir,
 Riding I had you, though you still staid there,
And in these thoughts, although you never stirre,
 You came with mee to Micham,[2] and are here.

1. Emblem Books; but the reading 'Fables' is found in authoritative MS. copies. Trenchers were commonly embellished with maxims.
2. Donne lived at Mitcham, Surrey, 1605–9, and wrote regularly from this address to Goodyer.

TO MR ROWLAND WOODWARD[1]

Like one who'in her third widdowhood doth professe
Her selfe a Nunne, tyed to retirednesse,
So'affects my muse now, a chast fallownesse;

Since shee to few, yet to too many'hath showne
How love-song weeds, and Satyrique thornes are growne
Where seeds of better Arts, were early sown.

Though to use, and love Poëtrie, to mee,
Betroth'd to no'one Art, be no'adulterie:
Omissions of good, ill, as ill deeds bee.

For though to us it seeme, 'and be light and thinne,
Yet in those faithfull scales, where God throwes in
Mens workes, vanity weighs as much as sinne.

If our Soules have stain'd their first white, yet wee
May cloth them with faith, and deare honestie,
Which God Imputes, as native puritie.

There is no Vertue, but Religion:
Wise, valiant, sober, just, are names, which none
Want, which want not Vice-covering discretion.

Seeke wee then our selves in our selves; for as
Men force the Sunne with much more force to passe,
By gathering his beames with a christall glasse;

1. Too little is known about Woodward, who was one of Donne's best
friends and possibly the owner of the copy of his poems known as the
'Westmoreland' MS. He accompanied Wotton on the latter's first
embassy to Venice and was employed as a courier. On one occasion he
was intercepted and imprisoned by the Inquisition. In 1608 he is known
to 'have entered the service' of the Bishop of London. He died some
time before 1636.

So wee, If wee into our selves will turne,
Blowing our sparkes of vertue, may outburne
The straw, which doth about our hearts sojourne.

You know, Physitians, when they would infuse
Into any'oyle, the Soules of Simples, use
Places, where they may lie still warme, to chuse.

So workes retirednesse in us; To rome
Giddily, and be every where, but at home,
Such freedome doth a banishment become.

Wee are but farmers of our selves, yet may,
If we can stocke our selves, and thrive, uplay
Much, much deare treasure for the great rent day.

Manure thy selfe then, to thy selfe be'approv'd,
And with vaine outward things be no more mov'd,
But to know, that I love thee'and would be lov'd.

TO SIR HENRY WOOTTON

Here's no more newes, than vertue,'I may as well
Tell you *Cales*,[1] or *Saint Michaels* tale for newes, as tell
That vice doth here habitually dwell.

Yet, as to'get stomachs, we walke up and downe,
And toyle to sweeten rest, so, may God frowne,
If, but to loth both, I haunt Court, or Towne.

For here no one is from the'extremitie
Of vice, by any other reason free,
But that the next to'him, still, is worse than hee.

1. *i.e.* Cadiz (not Calais) and the Azores. An allusion to the Islands' Voyage.

In this worlds warfare, they whom rugged Fate,
(Gods Commissary,) doth so throughly hate,
As in'the Courts Squadron to marshall their state:

If they stand arm'd with seely honesty,
With wishing prayers, and neat integritie,
Like Indians'gainst Spanish hosts they bee.

Suspitious boldnesse to this place belongs,
And to'have as many eares as all have tongues;
Tender to know, tough to acknowledge wrongs.

Beleeve mee Sir, in my youths giddiest dayes,
When to be like the Court, was a playes praise,
Playes were not so like Courts, as Courts'are like playes.

Then let us at these mimicke antiques jeast,
Whose deepest projects, and egregious gests
Are but dull Moralls of a game at Chests.

But now'tis incongruity to smile,
Therefore I end; and bid farewell a while,
At Court; though *From Court*, were the better stile.

TO THE COUNTESSE OF BEDFORD[1]

MADAME,
Reason is our Soules left hand, Faith her right,
By these wee reach divinity, that's you;
Their loves, who have the blessings of your light,
Grew from their reason, mine from faire faith grew.

1. Lucy, daughter of Lord Harington, married, 1594, Edward Russell,
3rd Earl of Bedford, and died, childless, 1627. The poets of her day were
her children and, besides Donne, who first met her in 1608, she befriended
and encouraged Ben Jonson, Chapman, Daniel, Drayton, and others.
'The Favourite of the Muses', she wrote poetry herself as well as inspired
it.

But as, although a squint lefthandednesse
Be'ungracious, yet we cannot want that hand,
So would I, not to encrease, but to expresse
My faith, as I beleeve, so understand.

Therefore I study you first in your Saints,
Those friends, whom your election glorifies,
Then in your deeds, accesses, and restraints,
And what you reade, and what your selfe devize.

But soone, the reasons why you'are lov'd by all,
Grow infinite, and so passe reasons reach,
Then backe againe to'implicite faith I fall,
And rest on what the Catholique voice doth teach;

That you are good: and not one Heretique
Denies it: if he did, yet you are so.
For, rockes, which high top'd and deep rooted sticke,
Waves wash, not undermine, nor overthrow.

In every thing there naturally growes
A *Balsamum* to keepe it fresh, and new,
If'twere not injur'd by extrinsique blowes;
Your birth and beauty are this Balme in you.

But you of learning and religion,
And vertue,'and such ingredients, have made
A methridate, whose operation
Keepes off, or cures what can be done or said.

Yet, this is not your physicke, but your food,
A dyet fit for you; for you are here
The first good Angell, since the worlds frame stood,
That ever did in womans shape appeare.

Since you are then Gods masterpeece, and so
His Factor for our loves; do as you doe,
Make your returne home gracious; and bestow
This life on that; so make one life of two.
    For so God helpe mee,'I would not misse you there
    For all the good which you can do me here.

TO THE COUNTESSE OF BEDFORD

MADAME,
You have refin'd mee, and to worthyest things
(Vertue, Art, Beauty, Fortune,) now I see
Rarenesse, or use, not nature value brings;
And such, as they are circumstanc'd, they bee.
    Two ills can ne're perplexe us, sinne to'excuse;
    But of two good things, we may leave and chuse.

Therefore at Court, which is not vertues clime,
(Where a transcendent height, (as, lownesse mee)
Makes her not be, or not show) all my rime
Your vertues challenge, which there rarest bee;
    For, as darke texts need notes: there some must bee
    To usher vertue, and say, *This is shee.*

So in the country'is beauty; to this place[1]
You are the season (Madame) you the day,
'Tis but a grave of spices, till your face
Exhale them, and a thick close bud display.
    Widow'd and reclus'd else, her sweets she'enshrines;
    As China, when the Sunne at Brasill dines.

Out from your chariot, morning breaks at night,
And falsifies both computations so;

1. *i.e.* Twickenham, Surrey, where Lady Bedford lived 1608–17.

Since a new world doth rise here from your light,
We your new creatures, by new recknings goe.
   This showes that you from nature lothly stray,
   That suffer not an artificiall day.

In this you'have made the Court the Antipodes,
And will'd your Delegate, the vulgar Sunne,
To doe profane autumnall offices,
Whilst here to you, wee sacrificers runne;
   And whether Priests, or Organs, you wee'obey,
   We sound your influence, and your Dictates say.

Yet to that Deity which dwels in you,
Your vertuous Soule, I now not sacrifice;
These are *Petitions*, and not *Hymnes*; they sue
But that I may survay the edifice.
   In all Religions as much care hath bin
   Of Temples frames, and beauty,'as Rites within.

As all which goe to Rome, doe not thereby
Esteeme religions, and hold fast the best,
But serve discourse, and curiosity,
With that which doth religion but invest,
   And shunne th'entangling laborinths of Schooles.
   And make it wit, to thinke the wiser fooles:

So in this pilgrimage I would behold
You as you'are vertues temple, not as shee,
What walls of tender christall her enfold,
What eyes, hands, bosome, her pure Altars bee;
   And after this survay, oppose to all
   Bablers of Chappels, you th'Escuriall.

Yet not as consecrate, but merely'as faire,
On these I cast a lay and country eye.

Of past and future stories, which are rare
I finde you all record, and prophecie.
  Purge but the booke of Fate, that it admit
  No sad nor guilty legends, you are it.

If good and lovely were not one, of both
You were the transcript, and originall,
The Elements, the Parent, and the Growth,
And every peece of you, is both their All:
  So'intire are all your deeds, and you, that you
  Must do the same thinge still; you cannot two.

But these (as nice thinne Schoole divinity
Serves heresie to furder[1] or represse)
Tast of Poëtique rage, or flattery,
And need not, where all hearts one truth professe;
  Oft from new proofes, and new phrase, new doubts
    grow,
  As strange attire aliens the men wee know.

Leaving then busie praise, and all appeale
To higher Courts, senses decree is true,
The Mine, the Magazine, the Commonweale,
The story of beauty,'in Twicknam is, and you.
  Who hath seene one, would both; As, who had bin
  In Paradise, would seeke the Cherubin.

TO THE COUNTESSE OF BEDFORD

On New-Yeares day

This twilight of two yeares, not past nor next,
  Some embleme is of mee, or I of this,
Who Meteor-like, of stuffe and forme perplext,

1. Obsolete form of 'further'.

Whose *what*, and *where*, in disputation is,
  If I should call mee *any thing*, should misse.

I summe the yeares, and mee, and finde mee not
  Debtor to th'old, nor Creditor to th'new,
That cannot say, My thankes I have forgot,
  Nor trust I this with hopes, and yet scarce true
  This bravery is, since these times shew'd mee you.

In recompence I would show future times
  What you were, and teach them to'urge towards such.
Verse embalmes vertue;'and Tombs, or Thrones of rimes,
  Preserve fraile transitory fame, as much
  As spice doth bodies from corrupt aires touch.

Mine are short-liv'd; the tincture of your name
  Creates in them, but dissipates as fast,
New spirits: for, strong agents with the same
  Force that doth warme and cherish, us doe wast;
  Kept hot with strong extracts, no bodies last:

So, my verse built of your just praise, might want
  Reason and likelihood, the firmest Base,
And made of miracle, now faith is scant,
  Will vanish soone, and so possesse no place,
  And you, and it, too much grace might disgrace.

When all (as truth commands assent) confesse
  All truth of you, yet they will doubt how I,
One corne¹ of one low anthills dust, and lesse,
  Should name, know, or expresse a thing so high,
  And not an inch, measure infinity.

1. In the sense of a small particle or grain.

I cannot tell them, nor my selfe, nor you,
    But leave, lest truth b'endanger'd by my praise,
And turne to God, who knowes I thinke this true,
    And useth oft, when such a heart mis-sayes,
    To make it good, for, such a praiser prayes.

Hee will best teach you, how you should lay out
    His stock of *beauty, learning, favour, blood;*
He will perplex security with doubt,
    And cleare those doubts; hide from you,'and shew you
      good,
    And so increase your appetite and food;

Hee will teach you, that good and bad have not
    One latitude in cloysters, and in Court;
Indifferent there the greatest space hath got;
    Some pitty'is not good there, some vaine disport,
    On this side sinne, with that place may comport.

Yet he, as hee bounds seas, will fixe your houres,
    Which pleasure, and delight may not ingresse,
And though what none else lost, be truliest yours,
    Hee will make you, what you did not, possesse,
    By using others, not vice, but weakenesse.

He will make you speake truths, and credibly,
    And make you doubt, that others doe not so:
Hee will provide you keyes, and locks, to spie,
    And scape spies, to good ends, and hee will show
    What you may not acknowledge, what not know.

For your owne conscience, he gives innocence,
    But for your fame, a discreet warinesse,
And though to scape, than to revenge offence

Be better, he showes both, and to represse
Joy, when your state swells, *sadnesse* when'tis lesse.

From need of teares he will defend your soule,
  Or make a rebaptizing of one teare;
Hee cannot, (that's, he will not) dis-inroule
  Your name; and when with active joy we heare
  This private Ghospell, then'tis our New Yeare.

TO THE COUNTESSE OF HUNTINGDON

MADAME,
Man to Gods image, *Eve*, to mans was made,
  Nor finde wee that God breath'd a soule in her,
Canons will not Church functions you invade,
  Nor lawes to civill office you preferre.

Who vagrant transitory Comets sees,
  Wonders, because they'are rare; But a new starre
Whose motion with the firmament agrees,
  Is miracle; for, there no new things are;

In woman so perchance milde innocence
  A seldome comet is, but active good
A miracle, which reason scapes, and sense;
  For, Art and Nature this in them withstood.

As such a starre, the *Magi* led to view
  The manger-cradled infant, God below:
By vertues beames by fame deriv'd from you,
  May apt soules, and the worst may, vertue know.

If the worlds age, and death be argued well
  By the Sunnes fall, which now towards earth doth bend,
  Then we might feare that vertue, since she fell
  So low as woman, should be neare her end.

But she's not stoop'd, but rais'd; exil'd by men
  She fled to heaven, that's heavenly things, that's you;
She was in all men, thinly scatter'd then,
  But now amass'd, contracted in a few.

She guilded us: But you are gold, and Shee;
  Us she inform'd, but transubstantiates you;
Soft dispositions which ductile bee,
  Elixarlike, she makes not cleane, but new.

Though you a wifes and mothers name retaine,
  'Tis not a woman, for all are not soe,
But vertue having made you vertue,'is faine
  T'adhere in these names, her and you to show,

Else, being alike pure, wee should neither see;
  As, water being into ayre rarify'd,
Neither appeare, till in one cloud they bee,
  So, for our sakes you do low names abide;

Taught by great constellations, which being fram'd,
  Of the most starres, take low names, *Crab*, and *Bull*,
When single planets by the *Gods* are nam'd,
  You covet not great names, of great things full.

So you, as woman, one doth comprehend,
  And in the vaile of kindred others see;
To some ye are reveal'd, as in a friend,
  And as a vertuous Prince farre off, to mee.

To whom, because from you all vertues flow,
   And 'tis not none, to dare contemplate you,
I, which doe so, as your true subject owe
   Some tribute for that, so these lines are due.

If you can thinke these flatteries, they are,
   For then your judgement is below my praise,
If they were so, oft, flatteries worke as farre,
   As Counsels, and as farre th'endeavour raise.

So my ill reaching you might there grow good,
   But I remaine a poyson'd fountaine still;
But not your beauty, vertue, knowledge, blood
   Are more above all flattery, than my will.

And if I flatter any,'tis not you
   But my owne judgement, who did long agoe
Pronounce, that all these praises should be true,
   And vertue should your beauty,'and birth outgrow.

Now that my prophesies are all fulfill'd,
   Rather than God should not be honour'd too,
And all these gifts confess'd, which hee instill'd,
   Your selfe were bound to say that which I doe.

So I, but your Recorder am in this,
   Or mouth, or Speaker of the universe,
A ministeriall Notary, for'tis
   Not I, but you and fame, that make this verse;

I was your Prophet in your yonger dayes,
And now your Chaplaine, God in you to praise.

TO MR T[HOMAS]. W[OODWARD].[1]

At once, from hence, my lines and I depart,
I to my soft still walks, they to my Heart;
I to the Nurse, they to the child of Art;

Yet as a firme house, though the Carpenter
Perish, doth stand: As an Embassadour
Lyes safe, how e'r his king be in danger:

So, though I languish, prest with Melancholy,
My verse, the strict Map of my misery,
Shall live to see that, for whose want I dye.

Therefore I envie them, and doe repent,
That from unhappy mee, things happy'are sent;
Yet as a Picture, or bare Sacrament,
 Accept these lines, and if in them there be
 Merit of love, bestow that love on mee.

TO MR E[DWARD]. G[ILPIN?].[2]

Even as lame things thirst their perfection, so
The slimy rimes bred in our vale below,
Bearing with them much of my love and hart,
Fly unto that Parnassus, where thou art.
There thou oreseest London: Here I have beene,
By staying in London, too much overseene.

1. It is assumed that the superscribed initials of this 'verse letter', as well
   as of three others, are those of a member of the Woodward family.
   Nothing is known about Thomas Woodward beyond the inference that
   he was an occasional poet.
2. Possibly the author of *Skialetbia*, 1598, or a member of the Goodyer
   family.

Now pleasures dearth our City doth posses,
Our Theatres are fill'd with emptines;
As lancke and thin is every street and way
As a woman deliver'd yesterday.
Nothing whereat to laugh my spleen espyes
But bearbaitings or Law exercise.
Therefore I'le leave it, and in the Country strive
Pleasure, now fled from London, to retrive.
Do thou so too: and fill not like a Bee
Thy thighs with hony, but as plenteously
As Russian Marchants, thy selfes whole vessel load,
And then at Winter retaile it here abroad.
Blesse us with Suffolks Sweets; and as it is
Thy garden, make thy hive and warehouse this.

TO MR R[OWLAND]. W[OODWARD].

If, as mine is, thy life a slumber be,
  Seeme, when thou read'st these lines, to dreame of me,
Never did Morpheus nor his brother weare
  Shapes soe like those Shapes, whom they would appeare,
As this my letter is like me, for it
  Hath my name, words, hand, feet, heart, minde and wit;
It is my deed of gift of mee to thee,
  It is my Will, my selfe the Legacie.
So thy retyrings I love, yea envie,
  Bred in thee by a wise melancholy,
That I rejoyce, that unto where thou art,
  Though I stay here, I can thus send my heart,
As kindly'as any enamored Patient
  His Picture to his absent Love hath sent.

All newes I thinke sooner reach thee than mee;
  Havens are Heavens, and Ships wing'd Angels be,

The which both Gospell, and sterne threatnings bring;
  Guyanaes harvest is nip'd in the spring,[1]
I feare; And with us (me thinkes) Fate deales so
  As with the Jewes guide God did; he did show
Him the rich land, but bar'd his entry in:
  Oh, slownes is our punishment and sinne.
Perchance, these Spanish businesse[2] being done,
  Which as the Earth betweene the Moone and Sun
Eclipse the light which Guyana would give,
  Our discontinued hopes we shall retrive:
But if (as all th'All must) hopes smoake away,
  Is not Almightie Vertue 'an India?

If men be worlds, there is in every one
  Some thing to answere in some proportion
All the worlds riches: And in good men, this,
  Vertue, our formes forme and our soules soule, is.

TO MR I. L.[3]

Of that short Roll of friends writ in my heart
  Which with thy name begins, since their depart,
Whether in the English Provinces they be,
  Or drinke of Po, Sequan, or Danubie,
There's none that sometimes greets us not, and yet
  Your Trent is Lethe', that past, us you forget.
You doe not duties of Societies,
  If from the'embrace of a lov'd wife you rise,
View your fat Beasts, stretch'd Barnes, and labour'd fields,
  Eate, play, ryde, take all joyes which all day yeelds,

1. An allusion to Ralegh's disappointed hopes of the Government under-
taking a settlement in Guiana c. 1596–7.
2. Singular form with plural meaning.
3. Apart from the inference that he resided and farmed in the north country,
nothing is known about the friend to whom Donne addressed this and
the following poem.

And then againe to your embracements goe:
   Some houres on us your frends, and some bestow
Upon your Muse, else both wee shall repent,
   I that my love, she that her guifts on you are spent.

TO MR I. L.

Blest are your North parts, for all this long time
   My Sun is with you, cold and darke'is our Clime;
Heavens Sun, which staid so long from us this yeare,
   Staid in your North (I thinke) for she was there,
And hether by kinde nature drawne from thence,
   Here rages, chafes, and threatens pestilence;
Yet I, as long as shee from hence doth staie,
   Thinke this no South, no Sommer, nor no day.
With thee my kinde and unkinde heart is run,
   There sacrifice it to that beauteous Sun:
And since thou art in Paradise and need'st crave
   No joyes addition, helpe thy friend to save.
So may thy pastures with their flowery feasts,
   As suddenly as Lard, fat thy leane beasts;
So may thy woods oft poll'd, yet ever weare
   A greene, and when thee list, a golden haire;
So may all thy sheepe bring forth Twins; and so
   In chace and race may thy horse all out goe;
So may thy love and courage ne'r be cold;
   Thy Sonne ne'r Ward; Thy lov'd wife ne'r seem old;
But maist thou wish great things, and them attaine,
   As thou telst her, and none but her, my paine.

TO SIR H[ENRY]. W[OTTON].

AT HIS GOING AMBASSADOR
TO VENICE [JULY 1604][1]

After those reverend papers, whose soule is
    Our good and great Kings lov'd hand and fear'd name,
By which to you he derives much of his,
    And (how he may) makes you almost the same,

A Taper of his Torch, a copie writ
    From his Originall, and a faire beame
Of the same warme, and dazeling Sun, though it
    Must in another Sphere his vertue streame:

After those learned papers which your hand
    Hath stor'd with notes of use and pleasure too,
From which rich treasury you may command
    Fit matter whether you will write or doe:

After those loving papers, where friends send
    With glad griefe, to your Sea-ward steps, farewel,
Which thicken on you now, as prayers ascend
    To heaven in troupes at'a good mans passing bell:

Admit this honest paper, and allow
    It such an audience as your selfe would aske;
What you must say at Venice this meanes now,
    And hath for nature, what you have for taske:

To sweare much love, not to be chang'd before
    Honour alone will to your fortune fit;
Nor shall I then honour your fortune, more
    Than I have done your honour wanting it.

1. Wotton was ambassador at Venice, on and off, for twenty years.

But'tis an easier load (though both oppresse)
    To want, than governe greatnesse, for wee are
In that, our owne and onely businesse,
    In this, wee must for others vices care;

'Tis therefore well your spirits now are plac'd
    In their last Furnace, in activity;
Which fits them (Schooles and Courts and Warres o'rpast)
    To touch and test in any best degree.

For mee, (if there be such a thing as I)
    Fortune (if there be such a thing as shee)
Spies that I beare so well her tyranny,
    That she thinks nothing else so fit for mee;

But though she part us, to heare my oft prayers
    For your increase, God is as neere mee here;
And to send you what I shall begge, his staires
    In length and ease are alike every where.

TO THE COUNTESSE OF BEDFORD

Honour is so sublime perfection,
And so refinde; that when God was alone
And creaturelesse at first, himselfe had none;

But as of the elements, these which wee tread,
Produce all things with which wee'are joy'd or fed,
And, those are barren both above our head:

So from low persons doth all honour flow;
Kings, whom they would have honoured, to us show,
And but *direct* our honour, not *bestow*.

For when from herbs the pure part must be wonne
From grosse, by Stilling, this is better done
By despis'd dung, than by the fire or Sunne.

Care not then, Madame,'how low your praysers lye;
In labourers balads oft more piety
God findes, than in *Te Deums* melodie.

And, ordinance rais'd on Towers, so many mile
Send not their voice, nor last so long a while
As fires from th'earths low vaults in *Sicil* Isle.

Should I say I liv'd darker than were true,
Your radiation can all clouds subdue;
But one,'tis best light to contemplate you.

You, for whose body God made better clay,
Or tooke Soules stuffe such as shall late decay,
Or such as needs small change at the last day.

This, as an Amber drop enwraps a Bee,
Covering discovers your quicke Soule; that we
May in your through-shine front your hearts thoughts see.

You teach (though wee learne not) a thing unknowne
To our late times, the use of specular stone,
Through which all things within without were shown.

Of such were Temples; so and of such you are;
Beeing and *seeming* is your equall care,
And *vertues* whole *summe* is but *know* and *dare*.

But as our Soules of growth and Soules of sense
Have birthright of our reasons Soule, yet hence
They fly not from that, nor seeke presidence:

Natures first lesson, so, discretion
Must not grudge zeale a place, nor yet keepe none,
Not banish it selfe, nor religion.

Discretion is a wisemans Soule, and so
Religion is a Christians, and you know
How these are one; her *yea*, is not her *no*.

Nor may we hope to sodder still and knit
These two, and dare to breake them; nor must wit
Be colleague to religion, but be it.

In those poor types of God (round circles) so
Religious tipes, the peecelesse centers flow,
And are in all the lines which all wayes goe.

If either ever wrought in you alone
Or principally, then religion
Wrought your ends, and your wayes discretion.

Goe thither stil, goe the same way you went,
Who so would change, do covet or repent;
Neither can reach you, great and innocent.

ANNIVERSARIES, EPICEDES
AND OBSEQUIES

Extract from
THE FIRST ANNIVERSARIE[1]
AN ANATOMY OF THE WORLD

What life the world hath stil.

For there's a kinde of World remaining still,
Though shee which did inanimate and fill
The world, be gone, yet in this last long night,
Her Ghost doth walke; that is, a glimmering light,
A faint weake love of vertue, and of good,
Reflects from her, on them which understood
Her worth; and though she have shut in all day,
The twilight of her memory doth stay;
Which, from the carcasse of the old world, free,
Creates a new world, and new creatures bee
Produc'd: the matter and the stuffe of this,
Her vertue, and the forme our practice is:
And though to be thus elemented, arme
These creatures, from home-borne intrinsique harme,
(For all assum'd unto this dignitie,
So many weedlesse Paradises bee,
Which of themselves produce no venemous sinne,
Except some forraine Serpent bring it in)

1. The subject of the two long and extravagant elegies, from which the
following extracts have been made, was Elizabeth, only child of Sir
Robert Drury of Hawstead, *co.* Suffolk, who died, aged fifteen, in 1610.
Donne had never met her, but her father was so moved by the eulogy
with which he celebrated the first anniversary of her death that he pro-
vided the poet and his family with rent-free accommodation in the
Drury mansion in Drury Lane. Donne refrained from repaying this wel-
come hospitality with an annual tribute after he had completed *The Second
Anniversarie*. Her epitaph, in Latin, in Hawstead Church was almost
certainly composed by him.

Yet, because outward stormes the strongest breake,
And strength it selfe by confidence growes weake,
This new world may be safer, being told   The sick-
The dangers and diseases of the old: nesses of
                                                           the world.
For with due temper men doe then forgoe,
Or covet things, when they their true worth know.
There is no health; Physitians say that wee,   Impossi-
At best, enjoy but a neutralitie.   bility of
                                                           health.
And can there bee worse sicknesse, than to know
That we are never well, nor can be so?
Wee are borne ruinous: poore mothers cry,
That children come not right, nor orderly;
Except they headlong come and fall upon
An ominous precipitation.
How witty's ruine! how importunate
Upon mankinde! it labour'd to frustrate
Even Gods purpose; and made woman, sent
For mans reliefe, cause of his languishment.
They were to good ends, and they are so still,
But accessory, and principall in ill;
For that first marriage was our funerall:
One woman at one blow, then kill'd us all,
And singly, one by one, they kill us now.
We doe delightfully our selves allow
To that consumption; and profusely blinde,
Wee kill our selves to propagate our kinde.
And yet we do not that; we are not men:
There is not now that mankinde, which was then,
When as, the Sunne and man did seeme to strive,
(Joynt tenants of the world) who should survive;   Short-
When, Stagge, and Raven, and the long-liv'd tree,   nesse of
                                                           life.
Compar'd with man, dy'd in minoritie;
When, if a slow pac'd starre had stolne away
From the observers marking, he might stay

Two or three hundred yeares to see't againe,
And then make up his observation plaine;
When, as the age was long, the sise was great;
Mans growth confess'd, and recompenc'd the meat;
So spacious and large, that every Soule
Did a faire Kingdome, and large Realme controule:
And when the very stature, thus erect,
Did that soule a good way towards heaven direct.
Where is this mankinde now? who lives to age,
Fit to be made *Methusalem* his page?
Alas, we scarce live long enough to try
Whether a true made clocke run right, or lie.
Old Grandsires talke of yesterday with sorrow,
And for our children wee reserve to morrow.
So short is life, that every peasant strives,
In a torne house, or field, to have three lives.
And as in lasting, so in length is man

Smalnesse of stature.

Contracted to an inch, who was a spanne;
For had a man at first in forrests stray'd,
Or shipwrack'd in the Sea, one would have laid
A wager, that an Elephant, or Whale,
That met him, would not hastily assaile
A thing so equall to him: now alas,
The Fairies, and the Pigmies well may passe
As credible; mankinde decayes so soone,
We'are scarce our Fathers shadowes cast at noone:
Onely death addes t'our length: nor are wee growne
In stature to be men, till we are none.

Extract from
THE SECOND ANNIVERSARIE
OF THE PROGRESSE OF THE SOULE

A just dis-
estimation
of the
world.

Forget this rotten world; And unto thee
Let thine owne times as an old storie bee.
Be not concern'd: studie not why, nor when:

Doe not so much as not beleeve a man.
For though to erre, be worst, to try truths forth,
Is far more businesse, than this world is worth.
The world is but a carkasse; thou art fed
By it, but as a worme, that carkasse bred;
And why should'st thou, poore worme, consider more,
When this world will grow better than before,
Than those thy fellow wormes doe thinke upon
That carkasses last resurrection.
Forget this world, and scarce thinke of it so,
As of old clothes, cast off a yeare agoe.
To be thus stupid is Alacritie;
Men thus Lethargique have best Memory.
Look upward; that's towards her, whose happy state
We now lament not, but congratulate.
Shee, to whom all this world was but a stage,
Where all sat harkning how her youthfull age
Should be emploi'd, because in all shee did,
Some Figure of the Golden times was hid.
Who could not lacke, what e'r this world could give,
Because shee was the forme, that made it live;
Nor could complaine, that this world was unfit
To be staid in, then when shee was in it;
Shee that first tried indifferent desires
By vertue, and vertue by religious fires,
Shee to whose person Paradise adher'd,
As Courts to Princes, shee whose eyes ensphear'd
Star-light enough, t'have made the South controule,
(Had shee beene there) the Star-full Northerne Pole,
Shee, shee is gone; she is gone; when thou knowest this,
What fragmentary rubbidge this world is
Thou knowest, and that it is not worth a thought;
He honors it too much that thinkes it nought.
Thinke then, my soule, that death is but a Groome,

Which brings a Taper to the outward roome,
Whence thou spiest first a little glimmering light,
And after brings it nearer to thy sight:
For such approaches doth heaven make in death.
Thinke thy selfe labouring now with broken breath,
And thinke those broken and soft Notes to bee
Division, and thy happyest Harmonie.
Thinke thee laid on thy death-bed, loose and slacke
And thinke that, but unbinding of a packe,
To take one precious thing, thy soule from thence.
Thinke thy selfe parch'd with fevers violence,
Anger thine ague more, by calling it
Thy Physicke; chide the slacknesse of the fit.
Thinke that thou hear'st thy knell, and think no more,
But that, as Bels cal'd thee to Church before,
So this, to the Triumphant Church, calls thee.
Thinke Satans Sergeants round about thee bee,
And thinke that but for Legacies they thrust;
Give one thy Pride, to'another give thy Lust:
Give them those sinnes which they gave thee before,
And trust th'immaculate blood to wash thy score.
Thinke thy friends weeping round, and thinke that they
Weepe but because they goe not yet thy way.
Thinke that they close thine eyes, and thinke in this,
That they confesse much in the world, amisse,
Who dare not trust a dead mans eye with that,
Which they from God, and Angels cover not.
Thinke that they shroud thee up, and think from thence
They reinvest thee in white innocence.
Thinke that thy body rots, and (if so low,
Thy soule exalted so, thy thoughts can goe,)
Think thee a Prince, who of themselves create
Wormes which insensibly devoure their State.
Thinke that they bury thee, and thinke that right

Laies thee to sleepe but a Saint Lucies night.
Thinke these things cheerefully: and if thou bee
Drowsie or slacke, remember then that shee,
Shee whose Complexion was so even made,
That which of her Ingredients should invade
The other three, no Feare, no Art could guesse:
So far were all remov'd from more or lesse.
But as in Mithridate, or just perfumes,
Where all good things being met, no one presumes
To governe, or to triumph on the rest,
Only because all were, no part was best.
And as, though all doe know, that quantities
Are made of lines, and lines from Points arise,
None can these lines or quantities unjoynt,
And say this is a line, or this a point,
So though the Elements and Humors were
In her, one could not say, this governes there.
Whose even constitution might have wonne
Any disease to venter on the Sunne,
Rather than her: and make a spirit feare,
That hee to disuniting subject were.
To whose proportions if we would compare
Cubes, th'are unstable; Circles, Angular;
She who was such a chaine as Fate employes
To bring mankinde all Fortunes it enjoyes;
So fast, so even wrought, as one would thinke,
No Accident could threaten any linke;
Shee, shee embrac'd a sicknesse, gave it meat,
The purest blood, and breath, that e'r it eate;
And hath taught us, that though a good man hath
Title to heaven, and plead it by his Faith,
And though he may pretend a conquest, since
Heaven was content to suffer violence,
Yea though hee plead a long possession too,

(For they're in heaven on earth who heavens workes do)
Though hee had right and power and place, before,
Yet Death must usher, and unlocke the doore.

Incommo-
dities of
the Soule
in the
Body.

Thinke further on thy selfe, my Soule, and thinke
How thou at first wast made but in a sinke;
Thinke that it argued some infirmitie,
That those two soules, which then thou foundst in me,
Thou fedst upon, and drewst into thee, both
My second soule of sense, and first of growth.
Thinke but how poore thou wast, how obnoxious;
Whom a small lumpe of flesh could poyson thus.
This curded milke, this poore unlittered whelpe
My body, could, beyond escape or helpe,
Infect thee with Originall sinne, and thou
Couldst neither then refuse, nor leave it now.
Thinke that no stubborne sullen Anchorit,
Which fixt to a pillar, or a grave, doth sit
Bedded, and bath'd in all his ordures, dwels
So fowly as our Soules in their first-built Cels.
Thinke in how poore a prison thou didst lie
After, enabled but to suck and crie.
Thinke, when'twas growne to most,'twas a poore Inne,
A Province pack'd up in two yards of skinne,
And that usurp'd or threatned with the rage
Of sicknesses, or their true mother, Age.
But thinke that Death hath now enfranchis'd thee,
Thou hast thy'expansion now, and libertie;

Her
liberty by
death.

Thinke that a rustie Peece, discharg'd, is flowne
In peeces, and the bullet is his owne,
And freely flies: This to thy Soule allow,
Thinke thy shell broke, thinke thy Soule hatch'd but
     now.
And think this slow-pac'd soule, which late did cleave
To'a body, and went but by the bodies leave,

Twenty, perchance, or thirty mile a day,
Dispatches in a minute all the way
Twixt heaven, and earth; she stayes not in the ayre,
To looke what Meteors there themselves prepare;
She carries no desire to know, nor sense,
Whether th'ayres middle region be intense;
For th'Element of fire, she doth not know,
Whether she past by such a place or no;
She baits not at the Moone, nor cares to trie
Whether in that new world, men live, and die.
Venus retards her not, to'enquire, how shee
Can, (being one starre) *Hesper*, and *Vesper* bee;
Hee that charm'd *Argus* eyes, sweet *Mercury*,
Workes not on her, who now is growne all eye;
Who, if she meet the body of the Sunne,
Goes through, not staying till his course be runne;
Who findes in *Mars* his Campe no corps of Guard;
Nor is by *Jove*, nor by his father barr'd;
But ere she can consider how she went,
At once is at, and through the Firmament.

ELEGIE ON THE LADY MARCKHAM[1]

Man is the World, and death th'Ocean,
    To which God gives the lower parts of man.
This Sea invirons all, and though as yet
    God hath set markes, and bounds, twixt us and it,
Yet doth it rore, and gnaw, and still pretend,
    And breaks our bankes, when ere it takes a friend.
Then our land waters (teares of passion) vent;

1. Bridget Harington (1579–1609), a first cousin of Lady Bedford, married
Sir Anthony Markham of Sedgebrook, *co.* Notts. Like Cecilia Bulstrode
she was a Gentlewoman of the Bedchamber to Queen Anne of Denmark,
and like her died at Twickenham Park.

Our waters, then, above our firmament,
(Teares which our Soule doth for her sins let fall)
    Take all a brackish tast, and Funerall,
And even these teares, which should wash sin, are sin.
    We, after Gods *Noe*, drowne our world againe.
Nothing but man of all invenom'd things
    Doth worke upon itselfe, with inborne stings.
Teares are false Spectacles, we cannot see
    Through passions mist, what wee are, or what shee.
In her this sea of death hath made no breach,
    But as the tide doth wash the slimie beach,
And leaves embroder'd workes upon the sand,
    So is her flesh refin'd by deaths cold hand.
As men of China,'after an ages stay,
    Do take up Porcelane, where they buried Clay;
So as this grave, her limbecke, which refines
    The Diamonds, Rubies, Saphires, Pearles, and Mines,
Of which this flesh was, her soule shall inspire
    Flesh of such stuffe, as God, when his last fire
Annuls this world, to recompence it, shall,
    Make and name then, th'Elixar of this All.
They say, the sea, when it gaines, loseth too;
    If carnall Death (the yonger brother) doe
Usurpe the body,'our soule, which subject is
    To th'elder death, by sinne, is freed by this;
They perish both, when they attempt the just;
    For, graves our trophies are, and both deaths' dust.
So, unobnoxious now, she'hath buried both;
    For, none to death sinnes, that to sinne is loth,
Nor doe they die, which are not loth to die;
    So hath she this, and that virginity.
Grace was in her extremely diligent,
    That kept her from sinne, yet made her repent.
Of what small spots pure white complaines! Alas,

How little poyson cracks a christall glasse!
She sinn'd, but just enough to let us see
    That God's word must be true, All, sinners be.
Soe much did zeale her conscience rarefie,
    That, extreme truth lack'd little of a lye,
Making omissions, acts; laying the touch
    Of sinne, on things that sometimes may be such.
As *Moses* Cherubines, whose natures doe
    Surpasse all speed, by him are winged too:
So would her soule, already'in heaven, seeme then,
    To clyme by teares, the common staires of men.
How fit she was for God, I am content
    To speake, that Death his vaine haste may repent.
How fit for us, how even and how sweet,
    How good in all her titles, and how meet,
To have reform'd this forward heresie,
    That women can no parts of friendship bee;
How Morall, how Divine shall not be told,
    Lest they that heare her vertues, thinke her old:
And lest we take Deaths part, and make him glad
    Of such a prey, and to his tryumph adde.

ELEGIE ON MISTRIS BOULSTRED [BULSTRODE][1]

Death I recant, and say, unsaid by mee
    What ere hath slip'd, that might diminish thee.
Spirituall treason, atheisme 'tis, to say,
    That any can thy Summons disobey.
Th'earths face is but thy Table; there are set

---

1. Cecilia Bulstrode (1584–1609), a Gentlewoman of the Bedchamber to Queen Anne, and a kinswoman of Lady Bedford. She was the subject of malicious gossip at Court and figures as the 'Court Pucelle' in a scandalous lampoon of Ben Jonson's. Jonson later made amends in an epitaph which was not however printed in his *Works*. Donne visited her on her early death-bed at Twickenham Park.

Plants, cattell, men, dishes for Death to eate.
In a rude hunger now hee millions drawes
  Into his bloody, or plaguy, or sterv'd jawes.
Now hee will seeme to spare, and doth more wast,
  Eating the best first, well preserv'd to last.
Now wantonly he spoiles, and eates us not,
  But breakes off friends, and lets us peecemeale rot.
Nor will this earth serve him; he sinkes the deepe
  Where harmlesse fish monastique silence keepe,
Who (were Death dead) by Roes of living sand,
  Might spunge that element, and make it land.
He rounds the aire, and breakes the hymnique notes
  In birds (Heavens choristers,) organique throats,
Which (if they did not dye) might seeme to bee
  A tenth ranke in the heavenly hierarchie.
O strong and long-liv'd death, how cam'st thou in?
  And how without Creation didst begin?
Thou hast, and shalt see dead, before thou dyest,
  All the foure Monarchies, and Antichrist.
How could I thinke thee nothing, that see now
  In all this All, nothing else is, but thou.
Our births and lives, vices, and vertues, bee
  Wastfull consumptions, and degrees of thee.
For, wee to live, our bellowes weare, and breath,
  Nor are wee mortall, dying, dead, but death.
And though thou beest, O mighty bird of prey,
  So much reclaim'd by God, that thou must lay
All that thou kill'st at his feet, yet doth hee
  Reserve but few, and leaves the most to thee.
And of those few, now thou hast overthrowne
  One whom thy blow makes, not ours, nor thine own.
She was more stories high: hopelesse to come
  To her Soule, thou'hast offer'd at her lower roome
Her Soule and body was a King and Court:

But thou hast both of Captaine mist and fort.[1]
As houses fall not, though the King remove,
   Bodies of Saints rest for their soules above.
Death gets 'twixt soules and bodies such a place
   As sinne insinuates 'twixt just men and grace,
Both worke a separation, no divorce.
   Her Soule is gone to usher up her corse,
Which shall be'almost another soule, for there
   Bodies are purer, than best Soules are here.
Because in her, her virtues did outgoe
   Her yeares, would'st thou, O emulous death, do so?
And kill her young to thy losse? must the cost
   Of beauty,'and wit, apt to doe harme, be lost?
What though thou found'st her proofe 'gainst sins of
     youth?
   Oh, every age a diverse sinne pursueth.
Thou should'st have stay'd, and taken better hold,
   Shortly, ambitious; covetous, when old,
She might have prov'd: and such devotion
   Might once have stray'd to superstition.
If all her vertues must have growne, yet might
   Abundant virtue'have bred a proud delight.
Had she persever'd just, there would have bin
   Some that would sinne, mis-thinking she did sinne.
Such as would call her friendship, love, and faine
   To sociablenesse, a name profane;
Or sinne, by tempting, or, not daring that,
   By wishing, though they never told her what.
Thus might'st thou'have slain more soules, had'st thou not
     crost
   Thy selfe, and to triumph, thine army lost.

1. *i.e.* Thou hast failed to overcome (missed) both 'King and Court' – the
ruler ('Captaine') and his protective 'fort'.

Yet though these wayes be lost, thou hast left one,
  Which is, immoderate griefe that she is gone.
But we may scape that sinne, yet weepe as much,
  Our teares are due, because we are not such.
Some teares, that knot of friends, her death must cost,
  Because the chaine is broke, though no linke lost.

DIVINE POEMS

LA CORONA[1]

1

Deigne at my hands this crowne of prayer and praise,
Weav'd in my low devout melancholie,
Thou which of good, hast, yea art treasury,
All changing unchang'd Antient of dayes;
But doe not, with a vile crowne of fraile bayes,
Reward my muses white sincerity,
But what thy thorny crowne gain'd, that give mee,
A crowne of Glory, which doth flower alwayes;
The ends crowne our workes, but thou crown'st our ends,
For, at our end begins our endlesse rest;
The first last end, now zealously possest,
With a strong sober thirst, my soule attends.
'Tis time that heart and voice be lifted high,
Salvation to all that will is nigh.

2

ANNUNCIATION

Salvation to all that will is nigh;
That All, which alwayes is All every where,
Which cannot sinne, and yet all sinnes must beare,

---

1. Grierson was the first of Donne's editors to suggest that this sequence of seven sonnets was sent to Magdalen Herbert. In a letter to her, dated 11 July, 1607, Donne had sent her, with an introductory sonnet, some 'holy hymns and sonnets' for her 'judgment and ... protection'. Walton, in his *Life*, assumed that 'these hymns are now lost; but doubtless they were such as they two now sing in heaven'.

Which cannot die, yet cannot chuse but die,
Loe, faithfull Virgin, yeelds himselfe to lye
In prison, in thy wombe; and though he there
Can take no sinne, nor thou give, yet he'will weare
Taken from thence, flesh, which deaths force may trie.
Ere by the spheares time was created, thou
Wast in his minde, who is thy Sonne, and Brother;
Whom thou conceiv'st, conceiv'd; yea thou art now
Thy Makers maker, and thy Fathers mother;
Thou'hast light in darke; and shutst in little roome,
Immensity cloysterd in thy deare wombe.

3

NATIVITIE

Immensity cloysterd in thy deare wombe,
Now leaves his welbelov'd imprisonment,
There he hath made himselfe to his intent
Weake enough, now into our world to come;
But Oh, for thee, for him, hath th'Inne no roome?
Yet lay him in this stall, and from the Orient,
Starres, and wisemen will travell to prevent
Th'effect of *Herods* jealous generall doome.
Seest thou, my Soule, with thy faiths eyes, how he
Which fils all place, yet none holds him, doth lye?
Was not his pity towards thee wondrous high,
That would have need to be pittied by thee?
Kisse him, and with him into Egypt goe,
With his kinde mother, who partakes thy woe.

4

TEMPLE

With his kinde mother who partakes thy woe,
Joseph turne backe; see where your child doth sit,
Blowing, yea blowing out those sparks of wit,
Which himselfe on the Doctors did bestow;
The Word but lately could not speake, and loe
It sodenly speakes wonders, whence comes it,
That all which was, and all which should be writ,
A shallow seeming child, should deeply know?
His Godhead was not soule to his manhood,
Nor had time mellowed him to this ripenesse,
But as for one which hath a long taske, 'tis good,
With the Sunne to beginne his businesse,
He in his ages morning thus began
By miracles exceeding power of man.

5

CRUCIFYING

By miracles exceeding power of man,
Hee faith in some, envie in some begat,
For, what weake spirits admire, ambitious, hate;
In both affections many to him ran,
But Oh! the worst are most, they will and can,
Alas, and do, unto the immaculate,
Whose creature Fate is, now prescribe a Fate,
Measuring selfe-lifes infinity to'a span,
Nay to an inch. Loe, where condemned hee
Beares his owne crosse, with paine, yet by and by
When it beares him, he must beare more and die.

Now thou art lifted up, draw mee to thee,
And at thy death giving such liberall dole,
Moyst, with one drop of thy blood, my dry soule.

6

RESURRECTION

Moyst with one drop of thy blood, my dry soule
Shall (though she now be in extreme degree
Too stony hard, and yet too fleshly,) bee
Freed by that drop, from being starv'd, hard, or foule,
And life, by this death abled, shall controule
Death, whom thy death slue; nor shall to mee
Feare of first or last death, bring miserie,
If in thy little booke my name thou enroule,
Flesh in that long sleep is not putrified,
But made that there, of which, and for which 'twas;
Nor can by other meanes be glorified.
May then sinnes sleep, and deaths soone from me passe,
That wak't from both, I againe risen may
Salute the last, and everlasting day.

7

ASCENTION

Salute the last and everlasting day,
Joy at the uprising of this Sunne, and Sonne,
Yee whose just teares, or tribulation
Have purely washt, or burnt your drossie clay;
Behold the Highest, parting hence away,
Lightens the darke clouds, which hee treads upon,
Nor doth hee by ascending, show alone.

But first hee, and hee first enters the way.
O strong Ramme, which hast batter'd heaven for mee,
Mild Lambe, which with thy blood, hast mark'd the
   path;
Bright Torch, which shin'st, that I the way may see,
Oh, with thine owne blood quench thine owne just wrath,
And if thy holy Spirit, my Muse did raise,
Deigne at my hands this crown of prayer and praise.

HOLY SONNETS

I

Thou hast made me, And shall thy worke decay?
Repaire me now, for now mine end doth haste,
I runne to death, and death meets me as fast,
And all my pleasures are like yesterday;
I dare not move my dimme eyes any way,
Despaire behind, and death before doth cast
Such terrour, and my feebled flesh doth waste
By sinne in it, which it t'wards hell doth weigh;
Onely thou art above, and when towards thee
By thy leave I can looke, I rise againe;
But our old subtle foe so tempteth me,
That not one houre my selfe I can sustaine;
Thy Grace may wing me to prevent his art,
And thou like Adamant draw mine iron heart.

V

I am a little world made cunningly
Of Elements, and an Angelike spright,
But black sinne hath betraid to endlesse night

My worlds both parts, and (oh) both parts must die.
You which beyond that heaven which was most high
Have found new sphears, and of new lands can write,
Powre new seas in mine eyes, that so I might
Drowne my world with my weeping earnestly,
Or wash it if it must be drown'd no more:
But oh it must be burnt! alas the fire
Of lust and envie have burnt it heretofore,
And made it fouler; Let their flames retire,
And burne me ô Lord, with a fiery zeale
Of thee and thy house, which doth in eating heale.

VI

This is my playes last scene, here heavens appoint
My pilgrimages last mile; and my race
Idly, yet quickly runne, hath this last pace,
My spans last inch, my minutes latest point,
And gluttonous death, will instantly unjoynt
My body, and soule, and I shall sleepe a space,
But my'ever-waking part shall see that face,
Whose feare already shakes my every joynt:
Then, as my soule, to'heaven her first seate, takes flight,
And earth-borne body, in the earth shall dwell,
So, fall my sinnes, that all may have their right,
To where they'are bred, and would presse me, to hell.
Impute me righteous, thus purg'd of evill,
For thus I leave the world, the flesh, and devill.

VII

At the round earths imagin'd corners, blow
Your trumpets, Angells, and arise, arise
From death, you numberlesse infinities
Of soules, and to your scattred bodies goe,

All whom the flood did, and fire shall o'erthrow,
All whom warre, dearth, age, agues, tyrannies,
Despaire, law, chance, hath slaine, and you whose eyes,
Shall behold God, and never tast deaths woe.
But let them sleepe, Lord, and mee mourne a space,
For, if above all these, my sinnes abound,
'Tis late to aske abundance of thy grace,
When wee are there; here on this lowly ground,
Teach mee how to repent; for that's as good
As if thou'hadst seal'd my pardon, with thy blood.

VIII

If faithfull soules be alike glorifi'd
As Angels, then my fathers soul doth see,
And adds this even to full felicitie,
That valiantly I hels wide mouth o'rstride:
But if our mindes to these soules be descry'd
By circumstances, and by signes that be
Apparent in us, not immediately,
How shall my mindes white truth by them be try'd?
They see idolatrous lovers weepe and mourne,
And vile blasphemous Conjurers to call
On Jesus name, and Pharisaicall
Dissemblers feigne devotion. Then turne
O pensive soule, to God, for he knowes best
Thy true griefe, for he put it in my breast.

IX

If poysonous mineralls, and if that tree,
Whose fruit threw death on else immortall us,
If lecherous goats, if serpents envious

Cannot be damn'd; Alas; why should I bee?
Why should intent or reason, borne in mee,
Make sinnes, else equall, in mee more heinous?
And mercy being easie, and glorious
To God, in his sterne wrath, why threatens hee?
But who am I, that dare dispute with thee?
O God, Oh! of thine onely worthy blood,
And my teares, make a heavenly Lethean flood,
And drowne in it my sinnes blacke memorie;
That thou remember them, some claime as debt,
I thinke it mercy, if thou wilt forget.

X

Death be not proud, though some have called thee
Mighty and dreadfull, for, thou art not soe,
For, those, whom thou think'st, thou dost overthrow,
Die not, poore death, nor yet canst thou kill mee.
From rest and sleepe, which but thy pictures bee,
Much pleasure, then from thee, much more must flow,
And soonest our best men with thee doe goe,
Rest of their bones, and soules deliverie.
Thou art slave to Fate, Chance, kings, and desperate men,
And dost with poyson, warre, and sicknesse dwell,
And poppie, or charmes can make us sleepe as well,
And better than thy stroake; why swell'st thou then?
One short sleepe past, wee wake eternally,
And death shall be no more; death, thou shalt die.

XI

Spit in my face you Jewes, and pierce my side,
Buffet, and scoffe, scourge, and crucifie mee,
For I have sinn'd, and sinn'd, and onely hee,

Who could do no iniquitie, hath dyed:
But by my death can not be satisfied
My sinnes, which passe the Jewes impiety:
They kill'd once an inglorious man, but I
Crucifie him daily, being now glorified.
Oh let mee then, his strange love still admire:
Kings pardon, but he bore our punishment.
And *Jacob* came cloth'd in vile harsh attire
But to supplant, and with gainfull intent:
God cloth'd himselfe in vile mans flesh, that so
Hee might be weake enough to suffer woe.

XIII

What if this present were the worlds last night?
Marke in my heart, O Soule, where thou dost dwell,
The picture of Christ crucified, and tell
Whether that countenance can thee affright,
Teares in his eyes quench the amazing light,
Blood fills his frownes, which from his pierc'd head fell.
And can that tongue adjudge thee unto hell,
Which pray'd forgivenesse for his foes fierce spight?
No, no; but as in my idolatrie
I said to all my profane mistresses,
Beauty, of pitty, foulnesse onely is
A signe of rigour: so I say to thee,
To wicked spirits are horrid shapes assign'd.
This beauteous forme assures a pitious minde.

XIV

Batter my heart, three person'd God; for, you
As yet but knocke, breathe, shine, and seeke to mend;
That I may rise, and stand, o'erthrow mee,'and bend

Your force, to breake, blowe, burn and make me new.
I, like an usurpt towne, to'another due,
Labour to'admit you, but Oh, to no end,
Reason your viceroy in mee, mee should defend,
But is captiv'd, and proves weake or untrue.
Yet dearely'I love you,'and would be loved faine,
But am betroth'd unto your enemie:
Divorce mee,'untie, or breake that knot againe,
Take mee to you, imprison mee, for I
Except you'enthrall mee, never shall be free,
Nor ever chast, except you ravish mee.

XVII

Since she whom I lov'd hath payd her last debt
To Nature, and to hers, and my good is dead,
And her Soule early into heaven ravished,
Wholly on heavenly things my mind is sett.
Here the admyring her my mind did whett
To seeke thee God; so streames do shew the head;
But though I have found thee, and thou my thirst has fed,
A holy thirsty dropsy melts mee yett.
But why should I begg more Love, when as thou
Dost wooe my soule for hers; offring all thine:
And dost not only feare least I allow
My Love to Saints and Angels things divine,
But in thy tender jealosy dost doubt
Least the World, Fleshe, yea Devill putt thee out.

XVIII[1]

Show me deare Christ, thy Spouse, so bright and clear.
What! is it She, which on the other shore

1. Donne alludes in this sonnet to the three divisions in the Church – Rome,
Geneva (including Germany) and England.

Goes richly painted? or which rob'd and tore
Laments and mournes in Germany and here?
Sleepes she a thousand, then peepes up one yeare?
Is she selfe truth and errs? now new, now outwore?
Doth she, and did she, and shall she evermore
On one, on seaven, or on no hill appeare?
Dwells she with us, or like adventuring knights
First travaile we to seeke and then make Love?
Betray kind husband thy spouse to our sights,
And let myne amorous soule court thy mild Dove,
Who is most trew, and pleasing to thee, then
When she'is embrac'd and open to most men.

XIX

Oh, to vex me, contraryes meet in one:
Inconstancy unnaturally hath begott
A constant habit; that when I would not
I change in vowes, and in devotione.
As humorous is my contritione
As my prophane Love, and as soone forgott:
As ridlingly distemper'd, cold and hott,
As praying, as mute; as infinite, as none.
I durst not view heaven yesterday; and to day
In prayers, and flattering speaches I court God:
To morrow I quake with true feare of his rod.
So my devout fitts come and go away
Like a fantastique Ague: save that here
Those are my best dayes, when I shake with feare.

GOOD FRIDAY, 1613.[1] RIDING WESTWARD

Let mans Soule be a Spheare, and then, in this,
The intelligence that moves, devotion is,
And as the other Spheares, by being growne
Subject to forraigne motions, lose their owne,
And being by others hurried every day,
Scarce in a yeare their naturall forme obey:
Pleasure or businesse, so, our Soules admit
For their first mover, and are whirld by it.
Hence is't, that I am carryed towards the West
This day, when my Soules forme bends toward the East.
There I should see a Sunne, by rising set,
And by that setting endlesse day beget;
But that Christ on this Crosse, did rise and fall,
Sinne had eternally benighted all.
Yet dare I'almost be glad, I do not see
That spectacle of too much weight for mee.
Who sees Gods face, that is selfe life, must dye;
What a death were it then to see God dye?
It made his owne Lieutenant Nature shrinke,
It made his footstoole crack, and the Sunne winke.
Could I behold those hands which span the Poles,
And tune all spheares at once, peirc'd with those holes?
Could I behold that endlesse height which is
Zenith to us, and to'our Antipodes,
Humbled below us? or that blood which is
The seat of all our Soules, if not of his,
Make durt of dust, or that flesh which was worne
By God, for his apparell, rag'd, and torne?
If on these things I durst not looke, durst I

1. 2 April. The title in one MS. copy is 'Riding to Sir Edward Herbert in
Wales'. Sir Edward Herbert, son of Magdalen Herbert, was the owner
at this date of Montgomery Castle.

Upon his miserable mother cast mine eye,
Who was Gods partner here, and furnish'd thus
Halfe of that Sacrifice, which ransom'd us?
Though these things, as I ride, be from mine eye,
They'are present yet unto my memory,
For that looks towards them; and thou look'st towards mee,
O Saviour, as thou hang'st upon the tree;
I turne my backe to thee, but to receive
Corrections, till thy mercies bid thee leave.
O thinke mee worth thine anger, punish mee,
Burne off my rusts, and my deformity,
Restore thine Image, so much, by thy grace,
That thou may'st know mee, and I'll turne my face.

A HYMNE TO CHRIST,

AT THE AUTHORS LAST GOING INTO GERMANY[1]

In what torne ship soever I embarke,
That ship shall be my embleme of thy Arke;
What sea soever swallow mee, that flood
Shall be to mee an embleme of thy blood;
Though thou with clouds of anger do disguise
Thy face; yet through that maske I know those eyes,
　Which, though they turne away sometimes,
　　They never will despise.

I sacrifice this Iland unto thee,
And all whom I lov'd there, and who lov'd mee;
When I have put our seas twixt them and mee,
Put thou thy sea betwixt my sinnes and thee.
As the trees sap doth seeke the root below
In winter, in my winter now I goe,
　Where none but thee, th'Eternall root
　　Of true Love I may know.

1. May 1619, as a member of Lord Doncaster's embassy.

Nor thou nor thy religion dost controule,
The amorousnesse of an harmonious Soule,
But thou would'st have that love thy selfe: As thou
Art jealous, Lord, so I am jealous now,
Thou lov'st not, till from loving more, thou free
My soule: Who ever gives, takes libertie:
   O, if thou car'st not whom I love
     Alas, thou lov'st not mee.

Seale then this bill of my Divorce to All,
On whom those fainter beames of love did fall;
Marry those loves, which in youth scattered bee
On Fame, Wit, Hopes (false mistresses) to thee.
Churches are best for Prayer, that have least light:
To see God only, I goe out of sight:
   And to scape stormy dayes, I chuse
     An Everlasting night.

A HYMNE TO GOD THE FATHER[1]

I

Wilt thou forgive that sinne where I begunne,
   Which is my sin, though it were done before?
Wilt thou forgive those sinnes, through which I runne,
   And do run still: though I still do deplore?
     When thou hast done, thou hast not done,
       For, I have more.

II

Wilt thou forgive that sinne by which I'have wonne
   Others to sinne? and, made my sinne their doore?

---

1. Composed during Donne's serious illness in the winter of 1623. According to Izaac Walton ' he caused it to be set to a most grave and solemn tune and to be often sung to the organ by the Choristers of St Paul's Church in his own hearing especially at the Evening Service . . . '.

Wilt thou forgive that sinne which I did shunne
　　A yeare, or two: but wallowed in, a score?
　　　When thou hast done, thou hast not done,
　　　　For I have more.

III

I have a sinne of feare, that when I have spunne
　　My last thred, I shall perish on the shore;
　　Sweare by thy selfe, that at my death thy sonne
　　　Shall shine as he shines now, and theretofore;
　　　　And, having done that, Thou haste done,
　　　　　I feare no more.

HYMNE TO GOD MY GOD, IN MY SICKNESSE[1]

Since I am comming to that Holy roome,
　　Where, with thy Quire of Saints for evermore,
　　I shall be made thy Musique; As I come
　　　I tune the Instrument here at the dore,
　　　And what I must doe then, thinke here before.

Whilst my Physitians by their love are growne
　　Cosmographers, and I their Mapp, who lie
　　Flat on this bed, that by them may be showne
　　　That this is my South-west discoverie
　　　Per fretum febris, by these streights to die,

I joy, that in these straits, I see my West;
　　For, though theire currants yeeld returne to none,
　　What shall my West hurt me? As West and East
　　　In all flatt Maps (and I am one) are one,
　　　So death doth touch the Resurrection.

1. Written, according to Izaac Walton, on 23 March 1630-1, eight days
before Donne's death. Sir Julius Cæsar in a note on a MS. copy dates it in
Donne's grave illness of 1623.

Is the Pacifique Sea my home? Or are
  The Easterne riches? Is *Jerusalem?*
Anyan, and *Magellan,* and *Gibraltare,*
    All streights, and none but streights, are wayes to them,
    Whether where *Japhet* dwelt, or *Cham,* or *Sem.*

We thinke that *Paradise* and *Calvarie,*
  Christs Crosse, and *Adams* tree, stood in one place;
Looke, Lord, and finde both *Adams* met in me;
    As the first *Adams* sweat surrounds my face,
    May the last *Adams* blood my soule embrace.

So, in his purple wrapp'd receive mee Lord,
  By these his thornes give me his other Crowne;
And as to others soules I preach'd thy word,
    Be this my Text, my Sermon to mine owne,
    Therfore that he may raise the Lord throws down.

Index of First Lines

MORE ABOUT PENGUINS
AND PELICANS

Penguinews, which appears every month, contains details of all the new books issued by Penguins as they are published. From time to time it is supplemented by *Penguins in Print*, which is a complete list of all titles available. (There are some five thousand of these.)

A specimen copy of *Penguinews* will be sent to you free on request. For a year's issues (including the complete lists) please send 50p if you live in the British Isles, or 75p if you live elsewhere. Just write to Dept EP, Penguin Books Ltd, Harmondsworth, Middlesex, enclosing a cheque or postal order, and your name will be added to the mailing list.

In the U.S.A.: For a complete list of books available from Penguin in the United States write to Dept CS, Penguin Books Inc., 7110 Ambassador Road, Baltimore, Maryland 21207.

In Canada: For a complete list of books available from Penguin in Canada write to Penguin Books Canada Ltd, 41 Steelcase Road, Markham, Ontario.

THE METAPHYSICAL POETS

Edited by Helen Gardner

Over half the poems chosen are from the great metaphysical poets, Donne, Herbert, Crashaw, Vaughan, and Marvell; but outside these the selection aims at presenting a wide range of poets who in varying ways show the influence of Donne and have written poems which merit the title 'metaphysical', from Sir Walter Raleigh to John Norris of Bemerton. In the introduction an attempt is made, not to define 'a metaphysical poem', but to describe some of the qualities which distinguish certain poets and poems in this period and make it necessary for us to regard them as forming to some degree a 'school of Donne', or what Johnson called 'a race of metaphysical poets'. Short biographical notes are provided and standard editions and biographies are noted. Notes explain any difficult words or unfamiliar ideas. The poems are edited from the original editions and the source of the text is given. The editor has tried to bear in mind the needs of the general reader to whom some of the common ideas of the seventeenth century are strange and also those of the student who needs a reliable text and to be referred to books in which further information can be found.

JOHN DONNE

THE COMPLETE ENGLISH POEMS

Edited by A. J. Smith

Donne's standing as one of the greatest poets in the English language is now thoroughly established, and critics such as T. S. Eliot, F. R. Leavis and William Empson have found in Donne's poetry qualities profoundly responsive to the modern age. His rhythms – once thought 'unmusical' – are a vigorous exploitation of the natural rhythms of the speaking voice, his 'eccentricity' represents a complex self-doubt and self-questioning, his 'obscurity' the reflection of a deeply subtle mind.

Until the publication of this volume no complete edition of Donne's verse has been available which made any serious and sustained attempt to help the reader appreciate the complexity and density of his poetry. A. J. Smith's annotation – which is very extensive, but critically aware – makes this edition an invaluable guide to a rewarding body of poetry: 'the purpose of this edition,' he writes, 'is to make an old and difficult author as intelligible as is now possible to readers of today'. Considerable attention has been paid to the text and a selection of the important manuscript variants are provided. This edition is also the first to make use of the newly discovered manuscript of the verse letter to Lady Carey and Mistress Essex Rich.

'It is clearly the best one volume edition available . . .' *The Times Literary Supplement*

A. J. Smith is Professor of English at the University of Keele.

THE LITERARY CRITICS

George Watson

SECOND EDITION

This remains the first complete history of English criticism by a British scholar since Saintsbury's, which is now over sixty years old. It is also highly original in approach. The author, who is a Cambridge lecturer in English, sees the development of criticism as a dynamic and uneven process. He dissociates himself from what he calls the 'Tidy School' of critical historians, which takes for granted a steady evolution of doctrine. Instead he traces a pattern broken up by sudden disturbances. The great critics refuse to accept obsolescent critical assumptions: they interrupt the commonplace literary debates of their day with their forcefully new ideas.

The Literary Critics forms a detailed illustration and development of this theme. It deals with English descriptive criticism – the analysis of literary works – from its origins in Dryden through the writings of the Augustans, Johnson, the Romantic critics, Arnold, and Henry James, to T. S. Eliot and the contemporary scene.

When it was first published *The Literary Critics* caused something of a stir, not least because of its astringent treatment of the critical stance of Dr F. R. Leavis, one of this country's most influential literary arbiters. In this new edition George Watson, in revising and updating his text throughout, has if anything sharpened his comments on the followers of T. S. Eliot.

A PELICAN BOOK

MYSTICISM:
A STUDY AND AN ANTHOLOGY

F. C. Happold

Mysticism is concerned with spiritual knowledge – the knowledge of truths we cannot understand with our minds. Most books on mysticism are difficult to follow without acquaintance with the writings of the mystics themselves, and the latter are hard to come by and too extensive for the ordinary reader.

This new book offers an original and effective solution of the difficulty. In it the author has combined both a study of mysticism, which makes its own contribution to the literature of the subject, and an anthology of mystical writings. Covering a wider field than previous selections, this anthology has been compiled to illustrate and complement the study. Its twenty-seven sections (each with an introductory note) are taken from the work not only of Christian mystics, but also from the *Upanishads* and the *Bhagavad Gita*, from Plato and Plotinus, and from the Sufi mystics of Islam.

In effect this forms a very simple and complete introduction to the vast range of mystical thought and speculation.

A PELICAN BOOK

PENGUIN MODERN POETS

This series is an attempt to introduce contemporary poetry to the general reader by publishing in a single volume a number of poems by each of three modern poets. Thirteen volumes have been published:

*NOT FOR SALE IN THE U.S.A.
†NOT FOR SALE IN THE U.S.A. OR CANADA

PENGUIN BOOKS OF VERSE

In addition to collections of Chinese, English, French (in four vols.), German, Greek, Irish, Italian, Japanese, Latin, Polish, Russian, South African, Spanish, and Welsh verse, Penguin Poets include the following specialized volumes:

ELIZABETHAN VERSE
introduced and edited by Edward Lucie-Smith

ENGLISH ROMANTIC VERSE
edited with an introduction by David Wright

GEORGIAN POETRY*
selected and introduced by James Reeves

POETRY OF THE THIRTIES*
introduced and edited by Robin Skelton

POETRY OF THE FORTIES*
introduced and edited by Robin Skelton

RESTORATION VERSE
introduced and edited by Harold Love

SATIRICAL VERSE
introduced and edited by Edward Lucie Smith

POETRY OF THE 'NINETIES
introduced and edited by R. K. R. Thornton

THE COMMON MUSE: POPULAR BRITISH BALLAD POETRY
FROM THE 15TH TO THE 20TH CENTURY*
introduced and edited by V. de Sola Pinto and A. E. Rodway

THE PENGUIN BOOK OF SOCIALIST VERSE
introduced and edited by Alan Bold

*NOT FOR SALE IN THE U.S.A.

YEVTUSHENKO
Selected Poems

Yevgeny Yevtushenko is the fearless spokesman of his generation in Russia. In verse that is young, fresh, and outspoken he frets at restraint and injustice, as in his now famous protest over the Jewish pogrom at Kiev.

But he can write lyrically, too, of the simple things of humanity – love, a birthday, a holiday in Georgia. And in 'Zima Junction' he brilliantly records his impressions on a visit to his home in Siberia.

THE PELICAN GUIDE TO ENGLISH LITERATURE

Edited by Boris Ford

What this work sets out to offer is a guide to the history and traditions of English literature, a contour-map of the literary scene in England. It attempts, in other words, to draw up an ordered account of literature that is concerned, first and foremost, with value for the present, and this as direct encouragement to people to read for themselves.

Each volume presents the reader with four kinds of related material:

    (i)   An account of the social context of literature in each period.

    (ii) A literary survey of the period.

    (iii) Detailed studies of some of the chief writers and works in the period.

    (iv) An appendix of essential facts for reference purposes.

The Guide *consists of seven volumes, as follows:*

1. THE AGE OF CHAUCER
2. THE AGE OF SHAKESPEARE
3. FROM DONNE TO MARVELL
4. FROM DRYDEN TO JOHNSON
5. FROM BLAKE TO BYRON
6. FROM DICKENS TO HARDY
7. THE MODERN AGE